SHILOH

OTHER YEARLING BOOKS BY PHYLLIS REYNOLDS NAYLOR
YOU WILL ENJOY:

ALL BUT ALICE
THE AGONY OF ALICE
ALICE IN RAPTURE, SORT OF
BEETLES, LIGHTLY TOASTED
MAUDIE IN THE MIDDLE
ONE OF THE THIRD GRADE THONKERS
THE BOYS START THE WAR/THE GIRLS GET EVEN

YEARLING BOOKS are designed especially to entertain and enlighten young people. Patricia Reilly Giff, consultant to this series, received her bachelor's degree from Marymount College and a master's degree in history from St. John's University. She holds a Professional Diploma in Reading and a Doctorate of Humane Letters from Hofstra University. She was a teacher and reading consultant for many years, and is the author of numerous books for young readers.

SHILOH

by Phyllis Reynolds Naylor

A Yearling Book

Published by
Bantam Doubleday Dell Books for Young Readers
a division of
Bantam Doubleday Dell Publishing Group, Inc.
1540 Broadway
New York, New York 10036

Visit us on the Web! www.bdd.com

Educators and librarians, visit the BDD Teacher's Resource Center at www.bdd.com/teachers

ISBN: 0-440-22811-5

Reprinted by arrangement with Macmillan Publishing Company, on behalf of Atheneum

Printed in the United States of America

July 1998

10   9   8   7   6   5   4   3   2   1

OPM

To Frank and Trudy Madden
and a dog named Clover

SHILOH

CHAPTER 1

The day Shiloh come, we're having us a big Sunday dinner. Dara Lynn's dipping bread in her glass of cold tea, the way she likes, and Becky pushes her beans up over the edge of her plate in her rush to get 'em down.

Ma gives us her scolding look. "Just once in my life," she says, "I'd like to see a bite of food go direct from the dish into somebody's mouth without a detour of any kind."

She's looking at me when she says it, though. It isn't that I don't like fried rabbit. Like it fine. I just don't want to bite down on buckshot, is all, and I'm checking each piece.

"I looked that rabbit over good, Marty, and you won't find any buckshot in that thigh," Dad says, buttering his bread. "I shot him in the neck."

Somehow I wish he hadn't said that. I push the meat from one side of my plate to the other, through the sweet potatoes and back again.

"Did it die right off?" I ask, knowing I can't eat at all unless it had.

"Soon enough."

"You shoot its head clean off?" Dara Lynn asks. She's like that.

Dad chews real slow before he answers. "Not quite," he says, and goes on eating.

Which is when I leave the table.

The best thing about Sundays is we eat our big meal at noon. Once you get your belly full, you can walk all over West Virginia before you're hungry again. Any other day, you start out after dinner, you've got to come back when it's dark.

I take the .22 rifle Dad had given me in March on my eleventh birthday and set out up the road to see what I can shoot. Like to find me an apple hanging way out on a branch, see if I can bring it down. Line up a few cans on a rail fence and shoot 'em off. Never shoot at anything moving, though. Never had the slightest wish.

We live high up in the hills above Friendly, but hardly anybody knows where that is. Friendly's near Sistersville, which is halfway between Wheeling and Parkersburg. Used to be, my daddy told me, Sistersville was one of the best places you could live in the whole state. You ask *me* the best place to live, I'd say right where we are, a little four-room house with hills on three sides.

Afternoon is my second-best time to go up in

the hills, though; morning's the best, especially in summer. Early, *early* morning. On one morning I saw three kinds of animals, not counting cats, dogs, frogs, cows, and horses. Saw a groundhog, saw a doe with two fawns, and saw a gray fox with a reddish head. Bet his daddy was a gray fox and his ma was a red one.

My favorite place to walk is just across this rattly bridge where the road curves by the old Shiloh schoolhouse and follows the river. River to one side, trees the other—sometimes a house or two.

And this particular afternoon, I'm about halfway up the road along the river when I see something out of the corner of my eye. Something moves. I look, and about fifteen yards off, there's this shorthaired dog—white with brown and black spots—not making any kind of noise, just slinking along with his head down, watching me, tail between his legs like he's hardly got the right to breathe. A beagle, maybe a year or two old.

I stop and the dog stops. Looks like he's been caught doing something awful, when I can tell all he really wants is to follow along beside me.

"Here, boy," I say, slapping my thigh.

Dog goes down on his stomach, groveling about in the grass. I laugh and start over toward him. He's got an old worn-out collar on, probably older than he

is. Bet it belonged to another dog before him.
"C'mon, boy," I say, putting out my hand.

The dog gets up and backs off. He don't even
whimper, like he's lost his bark.

Something really hurts inside you when you see
a dog cringe like that. You know somebody's been
kicking at him. Beating on him, maybe.

"It's okay, boy," I say, coming a little closer, but
still he backs off.

So I just take my gun and follow the river. Every
so often I look over my shoulder and there he is, the
beagle. I stop; he stops. I can see his ribs—not real
bad—but he isn't plumped out or anything.

There's a broken branch hanging from a limb
out over the water, and I'm wondering if I can bring
it down with one shot. I raise my gun, and then I
think how the sound might scare the dog off. I decide
I don't want to shoot my gun much that day.

It's a slow river. You walk beside it, you figure
it's not even moving. If you stop, though, you can see
leaves and things going along. Now and then a fish
jumps—big fish. Bass, I think. Dog's still trailing
me, tail tucked in. Funny how he don't make a sound.

Finally I sit on a log, put my gun at my feet, and
wait. Back down the road, the dog sits, too. Sits right
in the middle of it, head on his paws.

"Here, boy!" I say again, and pat my knee.

He wiggles just a little, but he don't come.

Maybe it's a she-dog.

"Here, girl!" I say. Dog still don't come.

I decide to wait the dog out, but after three or four minutes on the log, it gets boring and I start off again. So does the beagle.

Don't know where you'd end up if you followed the river all the way. Heard somebody say it curves about, comes back on itself, but if it didn't and I got home after dark, I'd get a good whopping. So I always go as far as the ford, where the river spills across the path, and then I head back.

When I turn around and the dog sees me coming, he goes off into the woods. I figure that's the last I'll see of the beagle, and I get halfway down the road again before I look back. There he is. I stop. He stops. I go. He goes.

And then, hardly thinking on it, I whistle.

It's like pressing a magic button. The beagle comes barreling toward me, legs going lickety-split, long ears flopping, tail sticking up like a flagpole. This time, when I put out my hand, he licks all my fingers and jumps up against my leg, making little yelps in his throat. He can't get enough of me, like I'd been saying no all along and now I'd said yes, he could come. It's a he-dog, like I'd thought.

"Hey, boy! You're really somethin' now, ain't

you?" I'm laughing as the beagle makes circles around me. I squat down and the dog licks my face, my neck. Where'd he learn to come if you whistled, to hang back if you didn't?

I'm so busy watching the dog I don't even notice it's started to rain. Don't bother me. Don't bother the dog, neither. I'm looking for the place I first saw him. Does he live here? I wonder. Or the house on up the road? Each place we pass I figure he'll stop—somebody come out and whistle, maybe. But nobody comes out and the dog don't stop. Keeps coming even after we get to the old Shiloh schoolhouse. Even starts across the bridge, tail going like a propeller. He licks my hand every so often to make sure I'm still there—mouth open like he's smiling. He *is* smiling.

Once he follows me across the bridge, though, and on past the gristmill, I start to worry. Looks like he's fixing to follow me all the way to our house. I'm in trouble enough coming home with my clothes wet. My ma's mama died of pneumonia, and we don't ever get the chance to forget it. And now I got a dog with me, and we were never allowed to have pets.

If you can't afford to feed 'em and take 'em to the vet when they're sick, you've no right taking 'em in, Ma says, which is true enough.

I don't say a word to the beagle the rest of the way home, hoping he'll turn at some point and go back. The dog keeps coming.

I get to the front stoop and say, "Go home, boy." And then I feel my heart squeeze up the way he stops smiling, sticks his tail between his legs again, and slinks off. He goes as far as the sycamore tree, lies down in the wet grass, head on his paws.

"Whose dog is that?" Ma asks when I come in. I shrug. "Just followed me, is all."

"Where'd it pick up with you?" Dad asks.

"Up in Shiloh, across the bridge," I say.

"On the road by the river? Bet that's Judd Travers's beagle," says Dad. "He got himself another hunting dog a few weeks back."

"Judd got him a hunting dog, how come he don't treat him right?" I ask.

"How you know he don't?"

"Way the dog acts. Scared to pee, almost," I say. Ma gives me a look.

"Don't seem to me he's got any marks on him," Dad says, studying him from our window.

Don't have to mark a dog to hurt him, I'm thinking.

"Just don't pay him any attention and he'll go away," Dad says.

"And get out of those wet clothes," Ma tells me. "You want to follow your grandma Slater to the grave?"

I change clothes, then sit down and turn on the TV, which only has two channels. On Sunday after-

17

noons, it's preaching and baseball. I watch baseball for an hour. Then I get up and sneak to the window. Ma knows what I'm about.

"That Shiloh dog still out there?" she asks.

I nod. He's looking at me. He sees me there at the window and his tail starts to thump. I name him Shiloh.

CHAPTER 2

Sunday-night supper is whatever's left from noon. If nothing's left over, Ma takes cold cornmeal mush, fries up big slabs, and we eat it with Karo syrup. But this night there's still rabbit. I don't want any, but I know Shiloh does.

I wonder how long I can keep pushing that piece of rabbit around my plate. Not very long, I discover.

"You going to eat that meat, or you just playing with it?" Dad asks. "If you don't want it, I'll take it for lunch tomorrow."

"I'll eat it," I say.

"Don't you be giving it to that dog," says Ma.

I take a tiny bite.

"What's the doggy going to *eat,* then?" asks Becky. She's three, which is four years younger than Dara Lynn.

"Nothing here, that's what," says Ma.

Becky and Dara Lynn look at Dad. Now I had *them* feeling sorry for the beagle, too. Sometimes girl-children get what they want easier than I do. But not this time.

"Dog's going right back across the river when we get through eating," says Dad. "If that's Judd's new dog, he probably don't have sense enough yet to find his way home again. We'll put him in the Jeep and drive him over."

Don't know what else I figured Dad to say. Do I really think he's going to tell me to wait till morning, and if the beagle's still here, we can keep him? I try all kinds of ways to figure how I could get that rabbit meat off my plate and into my pocket, but Ma's watching every move I make.

So I excuse myself and go outside and over to the chicken coop. It's off toward the back where Ma can't see. We keep three hens, and I take one of the two eggs that was in a nest and carry it out behind the bushes.

I whistle softly. Shiloh comes loping toward me. I crack the egg and empty it out in my hands. Hold my hands down low and Shiloh eats the egg, licking my hands clean afterward, then curling his tongue down between my fingers to get every little bit.

"Good boy, Shiloh," I whisper, and stroke him all over.

I hear the back screen slam, and Dad comes out on the stoop. "Marty?"

"Yeah?" I go around, Shiloh at my heels.

"Let's take that dog home now." Dad goes over

and opens the door of the Jeep. Shiloh puts his tail between his legs and just stands there, so I go around to the other side, get in, and whistle. Shiloh leaps up onto my lap, but he don't look too happy about it.

For the first time I have my arms around him. He feels warm, and when I stroke him, I can feel places on his body where he has ticks.

"Dog has ticks," I tell my dad.

"Judd'll take 'em off," Dad says.

"What if he don't?"

"It's his concern, Marty, not yours. It's not your dog. You keep to your own business."

I press myself against the back of the seat as we start down our bumpy dirt driveway toward the road. "I want to be a vet someday," I tell my dad.

"Hmm," he says.

"I want to be a traveling vet. The kind that has his office in a van and goes around to people's homes, don't make folks come to him. Read about it in a magazine at school."

"You know what you have to do to be a vet?" Dad asks.

"Got to go to school, I know that."

"You've got to have college training. Like a doctor, almost. Takes a lot of money to go to veterinary school."

My dream sort of leaks out like water in a paper

bag. "I could be a veterinarian's helper," I suggest, my second choice.

"You maybe could," says Dad, and points the Jeep up the road into the hills.

Dusk is settling in now. Still warm, though. A warm July night. Trees look dark against the red sky; lights coming on in a house here, another one there. I'm thinking how in any one of these houses there's probably somebody who would take better care of Shiloh than Judd Travers would. How come this dog had to be his?

The reason I don't like Judd Travers is a whole lot of reasons, not the least is that I was in the corner store once down in Friendly and saw Judd cheat Mr. Wallace at the cash register. Judd gives the man a ten and gets him to talking, then—when Mr. Wallace gives him change—says he give him a twenty.

I blink, like I can't believe Judd done that, and old Mr. Wallace is all confused. So I say, "No, I think he give you a ten."

Judd glares at me, whips out his wallet, and waves a twenty-dollar bill in front of my eye. "Whose picture's on this bill, boy?" he says.

"I don't know."

He gives me a look says, I thought so. "That's Andrew Jackson," he says. "I had two of 'em in my wallet when I walked in here, and now I only got one.

This here man's got the other, and I want my change."

Mr. Wallace, he's so flustered he just digs in his money drawer and gives Judd change for a twenty, and afterward I thought what did Andrew Jackson have to do with it? Judd's so fast-talking he can get away with anything. Don't know anybody who likes him much, but around here folks keep to their own business, like Dad says. In Tyler County that's important. Way it's always been, anyhow.

Another reason I don't like Judd Travers is he spits tobacco out the corner of his mouth, and if he don't like you—and he sure don't like me—he sees just how close he can spit to where you're standing. Third reason I don't like him is because he was at the fairgrounds last year same day we were, and seemed like everyplace I was, he was in front of me, blocking my view. Standin' in front of me at the mud bog, sittin' in front of me at the tractor pull, and risin' right up out of his seat at the Jorden Globe of Death Motorcycle Act so's I missed the best part.

Fourth reason I don't like him is because he kills deer out of season. He says he don't, but I seen him once just about dusk with a young buck strapped over the hood of his truck. He tells me the buck run in front of him on the road and he accidentally run over it, but I saw the bullet hole myself. If he got caught, he'd have to pay two hundred dollars, more than he's got in the bank, I'll bet.

We're in Shiloh now. Dad's crossing the bridge by the old abandoned gristmill, turning at the boarded-up school, and for the first time I can feel Shiloh's body begin to shake. He's trembling all over. I swallow. Try to say something to my dad and have to swallow again.

"How do you go about reporting someone who don't take care of his dog right?" I ask finally.

"Who you fixing to report, Marty?"

"Judd."

"If this dog's mistreated, he's only about one out of fifty thousand animals that is," Dad says. "Folks even bring 'em up here in the hills and let 'em out, figure they can live on rats and rabbits. Wouldn't be the first dog that wasn't treated right."

"But this one come to me to help him!" I insist. *"Knew* that's why he was following me. I got hooked on him, Dad, and I want to know he's treated right."

For the first time I can tell Dad's getting impatient with me. "Now you get that out of your head right now. If it's Travers's dog, it's no mind of ours *how* he treats it."

"What if it was a child?" I ask him, getting too smart for my own good. "If some kid was shaking like this dog is shaking, you wouldn't feel no pull for keeping an eye on him?"

"Marty," Dad says, and now his voice is just plumb tired. "This here's a dog, not a child, and it's not our dog. I want you to quit going on about it. Hear?"

I shut up then. Let my hands run over Shiloh's body like maybe everywhere I touch I can protect him somehow. We're getting closer to the trailer where Judd lives with his other dogs, and already they're barking up a storm, hearing Dad's Jeep come up the road.

Dad pulls over. "You want to let him out?" he says.

I shake my head hard. "I'm not lettin' him out here till I know for sure he belongs to Judd." I'm asking for a slap in the face, but Dad don't say anything, just gets out and goes up the boards Judd has laid out in place of a sidewalk.

Judd's at the door of his trailer already, in his undershirt, peering out.

"Looks like Ray Preston," he says, through the screen.

"How you doin', Judd?"

Judd comes out on the little porch he's built at the side of his trailer, and they stand there and talk awhile. Up here in the hills you hardly ever get down to business right off. First you say your howdys and then you talk about anything else but what you come for, and finally, when the mosquitoes start to bite, you say what's on your mind. But you always edge into it, not to offend.

I can hear little bits and pieces floating out over the yard. The rain . . . the truck . . . the tomatoes . . . the price of gasoline . . . and all the while Shiloh lays low in my lap, tail between his legs, shaking like a window blind in a breeze.

And then, the awful words: "Say, Judd, my boy was up here along the river this afternoon, and a beagle followed him home. Don't have any tags on his collar, but I'm remembering you got yourself another hunting dog, and wondered if he might be yours."

I'm thinking this is a bad mistake. Maybe it isn't Judd's at all, and he's such a liar he'd say it was, just to get himself still another animal to be mean to.

Judd hardly lets him finish; starts off across the muddy yard in his boots. "Sure as hell bet it is," he says. "Can't keep that coon dog home to save my soul. Every time I take him hunting, he runs off before I'm through. I been out all day with the dogs, and they all come back but him."

I can hear Judd's heavy footsteps coming around the side of the Jeep, and I can smell his chewing tobacco, strong as coffee.

"Yep," he says, thrusting his face in the open window. "That's him, all right." He opens the door. *"Git* on down here!" he says, and before I can even

26

give the dog one last pat, Shiloh leaps off my lap onto the ground and connects with Judd's right foot. He yelps and runs off behind the trailer, tail tucked down, belly to the ground. All Judd's dogs chained out back bark like crazy.

I jump out of the Jeep, too. "Please don't kick him like that," I say. "Some dogs just like to run."

"He runs all over creation," Judd says. I can tell he's studying me in the dark, trying to figure what's it to me.

"I'll keep an eye out for him," I say. "Anytime I see him away from home, I'll bring him back. I promise. Just don't kick him."

Judd only growls. "He could be a fine huntin' dog, but he tries my patience. I'll leave him be tonight, but he wanders off again, I'll whup the daylights out of him. Guarantee you that."

I swallow and swallow, and all the way home I can't speak a word, trying to hold the tears back.

CHAPTER 3

I don't sleep more than a couple hours that night. When I do, I dream of Shiloh. When I don't, I'm thinking about him out in the rain all afternoon, head on his paws, watching our door. Thinking how I'd disappointed him, whistling like I meant something that first time, gettin' him to come to me, then taking him on back to Judd Travers to be kicked all over again.

By five o'clock, when it's growing light, I know pretty much what I have to do: I have to buy that dog from Judd Travers.

I don't let my mind go any further; don't dwell on what Judd would want for Shiloh, or even whether he'd sell. Especially don't ask myself how I'm supposed to get the money. All I know is that I can think of only one way to get that dog away from Judd, and that's what I'm going to have to do.

My bed is the couch in the living room, so when Dad comes in to fix his breakfast, I pull on my jeans and go out to sit across from him in the kitchen.

First he makes himself a lunch to carry to work. He drives his Jeep to the post office in Sistersville, where he cases mail for around two hundred families and delivers it, then comes back to the Friendly post office where he cases mail for two hundred more. Delivers that, too. Route takes him 'bout eighty-five miles on roads you can hardly git by on in winter.

" 'Mornin'," he says to me as he stuffs a sandwich in a sack, then starts in on his breakfast, which is Wheat Chex and any fruit he can get from our peach tree. He makes himself coffee and eats the cornbread or biscuits Ma saves for him from our meal the night before.

"Can you think of a way I could earn myself some money?" I ask him, with this froggy kind of voice that shows you aren't woke up yet.

Dad takes another bite of cornbread, looks at me for a moment, then goes on studying his cereal. Says exactly what I figure he'd say: "Collect some bottles, take 'em in for deposit. Pick up some aluminum cans, maybe, for the recycling place."

"I mean real money. Got to have it faster than that."

"How fast?"

I try to think. Wish I could earn it in a week, but know I can't. Have to go out every day for a whole summer collecting cans and bottles to have much of anything at all.

"A month, maybe," I tell him.

"I'll ask along my mail route, but don't know many folks with money to spare," he says. Which is what I thought.

After Dad's gone off, Becky gets up before Ma, and I fix her a bowl of Cheerios, put her sneakers on so she won't stub her toes, and brush the snarls from her hair.

Read once in a book about how some kids earned money baby-sitting. Boy, if *I* ever got paid even a nickel for every time I've taken care of Becky—Dara Lynn, too—I'd have a lot of dollars. I do a whole bunch of jobs that other kids, other places, get paid to do, but it wouldn't ever occur to me to ask for pay. If I asked Dad, he'd say, "You live in this house, boy?" And when I'd say yes, he'd say, "Then you do your share like the rest of us."

Which is why I never asked.

"More Cheerios," says Becky, and all the while I'm making her breakfast, I'm thinking the best route to take to find aluminum cans. By the time Dara Lynn gets up, wearing one of Dad's old T-shirts for her nightgown, I'd figured how I could double my can count. But when Ma gets up a few minutes later, she takes one look at me and guesses what I'm thinking.

"You got that dog on your mind," she says, lifting the big iron skillet to the stove top and laying some bacon in it.

"Thinking don't cost nothing," I tell her.

She just gives me a little smile then and sets about making my bacon crisp, the way I like it, and we don't say any more about Judd's dog.

Must walk five miles that morning, and all I find is seven cans and one bottle. When Dad comes home about four, he hasn't found anybody looking for help, either, but he says, "The Sears fall catalog come in this afternoon, Marty. You got nothing better to do tomorrow, you could ride my route with me, help deliver 'em."

I say yes to that. Know I won't get nothing more out of it than a soft drink at the gas station, but I like going around in the Jeep, riding over back roads like Rippentuck and Cow House Run Road with Dad. Can take a bag with me just in case, pick up any cans or bottles I happen to see.

That night Dad and I sit out on the porch. Ma's in the swing behind us shelling lima beans for next day, and Becky and Dara Lynn's in the grass catching lightning bugs and putting 'em in a jar. Dad laughs at the way Becky squeals when she gits a bug in her hand. But seeing those bugs in a jar reminds me of Shiloh all chained up at Judd's, a prisoner as sure as those bugs. Truth is, about everything reminds me of Shiloh. You once get a dog to look at you the way Shiloh looked at me, you don't forget it.

"Got seventeen!" Dara Lynn shouts. "Aren't they pretty, Ma?"

"Almost could turn off the electricity and let 'em light the kitchen," Ma says.

"You going to let 'em go?" I ask.

Dara Lynn shrugs.

"They'll die if you keep 'em in a jar," I tell her.

Becky, she comes over and crawls onto my lap. "We'll let 'em go, Marty," she says, and kisses me on the neck. A butterfly kiss, she calls it. Bats her eyelashes against my skin, feels like a moth's wings. She laughs and I laugh.

Then far off I hear a dog. Leastwise I think it's a dog. Might could be a fox cub, but I think, Shiloh.

"You hear that?" I ask Dad.

"Just a hound complaining," is all he says.

Next morning Dad gives me a nudge when he comes through to the kitchen, and I'm up like a shot. We ride to Sistersville and I haul all those catalogs out to the Jeep while Dad cases mail. Not everybody gets a catalog, of course, but anyone who places an order with Sears during the year gets one, so there's lots to load up.

By quarter of nine, we're on the route; Dad pulls

the Jeep up close to the mailboxes and I stuff the mail in, turn up the little red flag on the side, if there is one. Some folks even wait down at the box, and then you feel real bad if you don't have anything for them.

Dad knows everybody's name, though, and he always takes time to say a little somethin'.

" 'Mornin', Bill," he says to an old man whose face lights up like Christmas when we stop. "How's the wife doing?"

" 'Bout the same," the man says, "but this catalog sure going to cheer her." And he sets off for his house, mail tucked under his arm.

People even leave somethin' in their boxes once in a while for Dad. Mrs. Ellison always leaves a little loaf of banana bread or a cinnamon roll, and Dad saves it to eat with his lunch.

After we finish Sistersville, we do the Friendly route, but as the Jeep gets up near Shiloh, my heart starts to pound. I'm thinking of closing my eyes tight in case the dog's around. If I see his eyes looking at me, they'll just drive me crazy. I can hear dogs barking when we're a half mile off from Judd Travers's trailer; dogs can pick up the sound of a Jeep that quick.

I get Judd's mail ready for him. He hasn't got any catalog coming, but he's got two other magazines that'll probably warm his heart—*Guns and*

Ammo and *Shooting Times.* Why don't he take a magazine about dogs, I'm thinking—teach him how to be kind?

All the dogs is chained when we get to his place, so none's waiting for us at the box. But Judd is. He's got a big old sickle; is cutting weeds along his side of the road.

" 'Mornin'," Dad says as the Jeep pulls up.

Judd straightens his back. His shirt's all soaked with sweat, and he wears this brown handkerchief tied around his forehead to keep the sweat from running in his eyes.

"How you doin', Ray?" he says, and comes over to the Jeep with his hand out. I give him his mail, and he even stinks like sweat. I know everybody sweats and everybody's sweat stinks, but seems to me Judd's sweat stinks worse than anyone's. Mean sweat.

"How come you aren't at work?" Dad says.

"You think this ain't work?" Judd answers, then laughs. "Got me a week of vacation coming, so I take a day now and then. This Friday I'm going hunting again. Take the dogs up on the ridge and see if I can get me some rabbit. Possum, maybe. Haven't had me a possum dinner for some time."

"Dogs okay?" Dad asks, and I know he's asking for me.

"Lean and mean," says Judd. "Keep 'em half
starved, they'll hunt better."

"Got to keep 'em healthy, though, or you won't
have 'em long," Dad says. I know he's saying that for
me, too.

"Lose one, I'll buy another," Judd tells him.

I can't help myself. I lean out the window where
I can see his face real good—big, round face, whisk-
ers on his cheeks and chin where he hasn't shaved his
face for five days—tight little eyes looking down on
me beneath his bushy brows.

"That dog that followed me home the other day,"
I say. "He okay?"

"He's learnin'," Judd says. "Didn't give him a
ounce of supper that night. Just put him where he
could watch the others eat. Teach him not to wander
off. Got him back in the shed, right now."

My stomach hurts for Shiloh. "That dog," I say
again. "What's his name?"

Judd just laughs, and his teeth's dark where the
tobacco juice oozes through. "Hasn't got a name.
Never name any of my dogs. Dogs one, two, three, and
four is all. When I want 'em, I whistle; when I don't,
I give 'em a kick. 'Git,' 'Scram,' 'Out,' and 'Dammit';
that's my dogs' names." And he laughs, making the
fat on his belly shake.

I'm so mad I can't see. I know I should shut

my mouth, but it goes on talking. "His name's Shiloh," I say.

Judd looks down at me and spits sideways. Studies me a good long time, then shrugs as the Jeep moves forward again and on along the river.

CHAPTER 4

"Marty," Dad says when we're around the bend, "sometimes you haven't got the sense to shut up. You can't go tellin' a man what to call his dog."

But I'm mad, too. "Better than callin' him 'Git' or 'Scram.'"

"Judd Travers has the right to name his dog anything he likes or nothing at all. And you've got to get it through your head that it's *his* dog, not yours, and put your mind to other things."

The Jeep bounces along for a good long mile before I speak again. "I can't, Dad," I say finally.

And this time his voice is gentle: "Well, son, you got to try."

I eat my peanut-butter-and-soda-cracker sandwiches with Dad at noon, plus the zucchini bread Mrs. Ellison had left in her mailbox for him, and after all the Sears catalogs and mail is delivered, we head back to the Sistersville post office. I get my Coca-Cola at the gas station while Dad finishes up, and we start home. I forget all about looking for cans

SHILOH

and bottles. The can I'm holding is the only one I got.

"Judd Travers goes hunting near every weekend, don't he?" I ask Dad.

"I suppose he does."

"You can shoot at just about anything that moves?"

"Of course not. You can only shoot at what's in season."

I'm thinking how, 'bout a year ago, I was fooling around up on the ridge and come across a dead dog. A dead beagle, with a hole in its head. Never said anything because what was there to say? Somebody out hunting got a dog by mistake, I figured. It happens. But the more I think on it now, I wonder if it wasn't Judd Travers shooting a dog on purpose— shooting one of his own dogs that didn't please him.

Dad's still talking: "We've got a new game warden in the county, and I hear he's plenty tough. Used to be a man could kill a deer on his own property anytime if that deer was eating his garden; warden would look the other way. But they tell me the new warden will fine you good. Well, that's the way it ought to be, I guess."

"What if a man shoots a dog?" I ask.

Dad looks over at me. "Dogs aren't ever in season, Marty. Now you know that."

"But what if a man shoots one, anyway?"

"That would be up to the sheriff to decide what to do, I guess."

The next day I start early and set out on the main road to Friendly with a plastic bag. Get me eleven aluminum cans, but that's all. Could walk my legs off for a year and not even have enough to buy half a dog.

The questions I'd tried not to think about before come back to me now. Would Judd Travers want to sell Shiloh at all? And how much would he want for him if he did? And even if I got Shiloh for my very own, how was I supposed to feed him?

There aren't many leftover scraps of anything in our house. Every extra bite of pork chop or boiled potato or spoonful of peas gets made into soup. If we'd had enough money for me to have a dog and buy its food and pay the vet and everything, I would have had one by now. Dara Lynn's been begging for a cat for over a year. It isn't that we're rock-poor; trouble is that Grandma Preston's got real feeble, and she's being cared for by Dad's sister over in Clarksburg. Have to have nurses anytime Aunt Hettie goes out, and every spare cent we got goes to pay for Grandma's care. Nothing left over to feed a dog. But I figure to get to that problem later on.

I wonder if maybe, in time, if I never see Shiloh again, I'll forget about him. But then I'm lying on

39

the couch that night after everyone else has gone to bed, and I hear this far-off sound again, like a dog crying. Not barking, not howling, not whining even. Crying. And I get this awful ache in my chest. I wonder if it *is* a dog. If it's Shiloh.

, "I know you want a dog, Marty," Ma says to me on Thursday. She's sitting at the kitchen table with cardboard boxes all around her, folding a stack of letters and putting them in envelopes. Ma gets work to do here at home anytime she can. "I wish we had the money so every one of you kids could have a pet. But with Grandma seeming to need more care, we just don't, and that's that."

I nod. Ma knows me better'n I know myself sometimes, but she don't have this straight. I don't want just any dog. I want Shiloh, because he needs me. Needs me bad.

It's Friday morning when I hear the sound. Dad's off on his mail route, Dara Lynn and Becky's watching cartoons on TV, Ma's out on the back porch washing clothes in the old washing machine that don't work—only the wringer part works if you turn it by hand. I'm sitting at the table eating a piece of bread spread with lard and jam when I hear the noise I know is Shiloh. Only the softest kind of noise—and right close.

I fold the bread up, jelly to the inside, stick it in

my pocket, and go out the front door. Shiloh's under the sycamore, head on his paws, just like the day he followed me home in the rain. Soon as I see him, I know two things: (1) Judd Travers has taken his dogs out hunting, like he said, and Shiloh's run away from the pack, and (2) I'm not going to take him back. Not now, not ever.

I don't have time to think how I had promised Judd if I ever saw Shiloh loose again, I'd bring him back. Don't even think what I'm going to tell Dad. All I know right then is that I have to get Shiloh away from the house, where none of the family will see him. I run barefoot down the front steps and over to where Shiloh's lying, his tail just thumping like crazy in the grass.

"Shiloh!" I whisper, and gather him up in my arms. His body is shaking all over, but he don't try to get away, don't creep off from me the way he did that first day. I hold him as close and careful as I carry Becky when she's asleep, and I start off up the far hill into the woods, carrying my dog. I know that if I was to see Judd Travers that very minute with his rifle, I'd tell him he'd have to shoot me before I'd ever let him near Shiloh again.

There are burrs and stickers on the path up the hill, and usually I wouldn't take it without sneakers, but if there's burrs and stickers in my feet, I hardly feel 'em. Know Judd Travers and his hounds won't be over here, 'cause this hill belongs to my dad. Get me as far as the shadbush next to the pine, and then I sit down and hug Shiloh.

First time I really have him to myself—first time I can hug him, nobody looking, just squeeze his thin body, pat his head, stroke his ears.

"Shiloh," I tell him, as though he knows it's his name, "Judd Travers isn't never going to kick you again."

And the way his eyes look at me then, the way he reaches up and licks my face, it's like it seals the promise. I'd made a promise to Judd Travers I wasn't going to keep, Jesus help me. But I'm making one to Shiloh that I *will*, God strike me dead.

I set him down at last and go over to the creek for a drink of water. Shiloh follows along beside me. I cup my hands and drink, and Shiloh helps himself, lapping it up. Now what? I ask myself. The problem is looking me square in the face.

I got to keep Shiloh a secret. That much I know. But I'm not going to keep him chained. Only thing I can think of is to make him a pen. Don't like the idea of it, but I'll be with him as much as I can.

I take him back to the shadbush and Shiloh lays down.

"Shiloh," I say, patting his head. "Stay!"

He thumps his tail. I start to walk away, looking back. Shiloh gets up. "Stay!" I say again, louder, and point to the ground.

He lays back down, but I know he's like to follow, anyways. So I pull him over to a pine tree, take the belt off my jeans, loop it through the raggedy old collar Shiloh's wearing, and fasten the belt to the tree. Shiloh don't like it much, but he's quiet. I go down the path and every so often I turn around. Shiloh is looking at me like he won't never see me again, but he don't bark. Strangest thing I ever see in a dog, to be that still.

Ma's still on the back porch. When she washes, it takes her near all day. Dara Lynn and Becky's stuck to the TV. So I go to the shed by the side of the house and I take the extra fencing Dad used when we had us more chickens. I take me a piece of wire, too, and go back up the hill.

Shiloh's still there, and he don't try to get up while I set to work. I string the fencing around the trunks of three small trees, for corner posts, and then back to the pine tree again where I fasten it with wire. Pen measures about six by eight feet.

I go back down to the shed again, and this time I get the old rotten planks Dad took out of the back steps when he put in the new. Pick me up an old pie tin, too. I take the planks up to Shiloh's pen and make him a lean-to at one end, to protect him from rain. Fill the pie tin with water so's he'll have something to drink.

Last of all, I take the lard bread from my pocket and feed it to Shiloh in little pieces, letting him lick my fingers after every bite. I wrap my arms around him, pat him, run my hands over his ears, even kiss his nose. I tell him about a million times I love him as much as I love my ma.

The worry part is whether or not he'll stay quiet. I'm hoping he will, 'cause he was a silent dog to begin with, but all the way back down the hill to the house, I put my finger to my lips and turn back.

"Shhh!" I say.

Shiloh, he don't make a sound. Like he had the bark beat out of him when he was a pup and it just never come back.

I'm tense as a cricket that night. Tense when Dad drives up in his Jeep, afraid the dog will bark. Tense when Dara Lynn and Becky are out in the yard playing after dinner, squealin' and yellin', afraid that Shiloh will want to get in on the fun and maybe dig a hole under the fence. He never comes.

I manage to take a piece of potato and some cornbread up to him before it gets dark. I sit down in his pen with him, and he crawls all over me, licking my face. If he'd been a cat, he would have purred, he was that glad to see me.

Tell him I'm coming back tomorrow with some kind of leash for him. Tell him we're going to run all over that hill, him and me, every day. Tell him he's my dog now, and I'm not never going to let anybody hurt him again ever, and then I leave, wiring that fence good. I go home and sleep a full night, first time in a long while.

CHAPTER 5

I got to take one problem at a time, I tell myself.

Problem number one: where to keep Shiloh hid. Solved.

Problem number two: Would Shiloh be quiet? Yes, he would.

Problem number three: How am I going to get food out of the house, enough to feed Shiloh twice a day, without Ma noticing?

The next morning before breakfast, as soon as Dad's gone, I take a biscuit from the kitchen and a rope from the shed outside, and run up the far hill before Ma and Dara Lynn and Becky get out of bed.

This time Shiloh's on his feet waiting for me, tail going like a windshield wiper, fast speed. A soft yip of pure joy cuts off quick when I say "Shhh!" but as soon as I'm in the pen, Shiloh's leaping up almost shoulder high to lick my cheek, nuzzling my hands, my thighs. He gulps down the biscuit I give him. Wants more, I can tell, but he don't bark. Seems to know he's safe only as long as he's quiet. I tie the rope to his collar.

"Shiloh, boy, we're goin' for a run," I tell him.

To get in and out of Shiloh's pen, I got to unfasten the piece of wire that holds the fencing against the trunk of the pine, then move the fencing aside long enough to slip out. Shiloh lets me go through first, he follows, and then we're both together, like a six-legged animal, pounding along up the path, legs bumping, Shiloh leaping up to lick my hand. I let go of the rope and let Shiloh run free for a while. If he goes ahead even a few steps, he stops and looks back to see if I'm coming; if he stops to sniff at a tree or bush and I go on by, his feet pound double time to catch up.

Just out of the woods on the other side of the hill, there's a meadow, and I slump down in the grass to rest. Shiloh's all over me, licking my face sloppy wet. I giggle and roll over on my stomach, covering my head and neck with my arms. Shiloh whines and nudges his nose under my shoulder, working to roll me over. I laugh and turn on my back, pulling Shiloh down onto my chest, and for a while we both lay there, panting, enjoying the sunshine, belonging to each other.

"What'd you do today, Marty?" Dad asks as he gets out of his Jeep late that evening.

"Oh, looked for ground hogs up on the hill. Fooled around," I tell him.

"How's the can collecting coming?"

"Found some a couple days ago."

"Saw some bottles in the ditch down near Doc Murphy's," Dad says.

"I'll go take a look," I tell him, and set out with my bag. I have to keep on collecting cans, enough to cover some money for meat and bones from the grocer down in Friendly. The bigger Shiloh grows, the more he'll eat.

When I get back home, supper's on the table, and I slip into my chair just as Dad asks the blessing: "Dear Lord, we thank you for the food you've provided for our table. Bless it to nourish the good within us. Amen."

Ma picks up the meat loaf and passes it around, and the meal begins.

I eat about half my supper, then say, "I been getting this sort of full feeling at dinner, Ma, and then I'm hungry again before I go to bed."

Ma don't even look up. "Well, don't eat so much at dinner, then, and eat again before bedtime."

"Food'll be all gone by then."

"There's always cornflakes or something."

"But I get hungry for meat and potatoes later."

"Save some back, then."

"Dara Lynn'll eat it."

"For goodness' sake, Marty!" says Ma.

"Who wants cold meat loaf?" Dara Lynn says.

Forks continue clinking on the table; Becky keeps on digging her fork in her boiled potato. No one looks up. No one pauses. No one even questions. Easy as falling off a log.

I get up from the table finally and put some of my meat loaf and half a potato on a saucer.

"I'm puttin' this in the fridge, Dara Lynn," I say. "Don't you go pickin' at it."

"I *won't,* I told you!" she says.

I go into the other room and sit down on the sofa. So far, so good.

"You seem restless, Marty," Ma calls.

"Me? Heck, no. I got lots to do."

"Where's David Howard this summer? Haven't seen him around."

"Think he went to Tennessee to visit his uncle."

"Fred? Michael?"

"Haven't seen Fred. Michael's gone to some kind of camp."

"You're not lonely?"

"How can I be lonely with the whole outdoors to play in?" I answer. Wish they'd get off my back.

"You can ride along to work with me again anytime you want," says Dad.

I pick up the comic book I bought a few weeks back. "I want to go, I'll let you know," I tell him.

Gradually the kitchen clatter dies down. Dad

belches and goes out on the back porch to look at the sky, same as he always does. Becky's fooling with her food, and Ma sends her away from the table. Dara Lynn giggles at Becky and gets asked to clear the dishes.

I wait until everyone is out of the kitchen and sitting around on the back porch to catch the breeze. As usual Becky and Dara Lynn whoop and tumble around in the grass, glad for an audience, and after I sit a respectable amount of time, I say, "Think I'll take my .22 and go up the far hill awhile."

"What you figure on shooting this time of evening?" Dad asks.

"Just workin' on my aim," I tell him. "See how good I can hit when the light's dim."

"Don't you ever, never, aim your gun toward this house or yard," Ma says.

"I'll point it dead away," I promise. I go back inside for my gun, slip the leftover food from the saucer into a little plastic sack, and set off up the hill, the sounds of my sisters' shouts and giggles behind me.

Again, as I get near the pen, I hear soft, happy yips. But soon as I say, "Shhh!" the noise stops. The only sound you can hear is the swishing of Shiloh's tail, hitting the fence, the soft pad of his paws as he leaps up in the air in sheer, pure happiness; the sloppy slap of his jowls together as he gobbles down the supper I've brought him and then he commences to slobber love all over me as well.

I unhook the wire, push the fence open, and lead Shiloh to the stream for a drink, filling the pie pan with fresh water. When I lead him back to the pen again, I can tell he's disappointed, wanted to go for a run, but I give him enough hugging and squeezing and petting to last the night, with the promise of another run through the meadow the next day.

I'm halfway down the hill when I remember I haven't fired my gun once, and wonder if Dad will say anything. By the time I reach the back porch, though, the whole family's facing down the driveway, 'cause there's the sound of a truck motor growing louder and louder.

I stop in my tracks, fingers tightening around my gun.

Dad, sitting on the edge of the porch, leans forward so he can see. "Looks like Judd Travers's pickup," he says.

My chest feels tight, like I'm having trouble breathing.

The truck pulls up by the side of the house, and the door swings open.

" Evenin'!" Dad calls out as Judd, wearing his old western-style boots with the sharp heel, gets out and comes over.

51

" Evenin'," he says.

"You had dinner?" Ma asks. "I got some left-
overs I could heat up real quick."

"Had me some ribs already," he says. "Ain't
looking for a meal, Mrs. Preston, I'm looking for a
dog." He sure don't waste any time getting to the
point. Now my heart's really pounding.

"That new dog of yours run off again?" Dad
asks him.

"I swear to God I find him this time, I'm goin'
to break his legs," Judd says, and spits.

"Oh, come on, Judd. A dog with four broke legs
ain't no dog to you at all."

"He's no dog to me at all the way he keeps runnin' off. It's the fourth time he's left the pack when
I had him out huntin'. I got to teach him a lesson.
Whup him good and starve him lean. Wondered if
you'd seen him."

"I sure didn't see him on my route today, and
you know if I had, I'd have put him in the Jeep and
brought him to you straight away," says Dad.

"What about that boy of yours? Think he's
seen him?"

Dad had heard me coming back from the hill,
and he turns around. "Marty?"

I stand rooted to the ground at the side of the
house. "What?"

"Come on around here. Judd's dog's missing again, and he wants to know have you seen him."

"H-his dog? Here in this yard? Haven't seen any dog of any kind in our yard all day," I say, coming a few steps closer.

Judd is sure studying me hard. So is Dad.

"Well, how about when you went out looking for bottles?" Dad asks. "You see him then?"

"Nope." My voice is stronger now. "Saw that big German shepherd of Baker's that gets loose sometimes, and saw a little old gray dog, but sure didn't see that beagle."

"Well, you keep an eye out sharp," Judd says, "and if you see him, you throw a rope around him, drag him over. Hear?"

I only look at him. Can't speak. Can't even nod my head. I wouldn't never promise him that.

"You hear what he asked you, Marty?" says Dad.

I nod my head. Yes, I heard, all right.

"Okay, then," Judd says, and gets back in his pickup.

"Have any luck hunting yesterday?" Dad calls after him.

"A rabbit. Saw a groundhog but didn't get it. That new dog hadn't run off, he would've got it for me. He wasn't such a good hunting dog, I would have shot him by now."

"Sheriff would get on you if you do somethin' like that, Judd."

"Law never told me before what I could do with my dogs, won't be tellin' me now," Judd says. He laughs, waves his hand, starts the engine, and the pickup pulls away.

CHAPTER 6

Night in West Virginia is as dark as black can be. No car lights sweepin' across my walls or ceiling like when I stay overnight with David Howard down in Friendly. No street lamps shinin' in the windows, no lights from next-door houses. Where I live, there ain't no street lamps at all, no house close enough to see from our windows.

My eyes are open, anyway. I stare up into the darkness of the living room and the darkness stares back.

I'm remembering how once, several years ago, when Ma bought milk chocolate rabbits one Easter for me and Dara Lynn, I'd finished eating mine, but Dara Lynn took only a nibble of hers every day or so, keeping it up on her dresser in its pink and yellow tinfoil, driving me nuts. And one day I just crept in there and ate off one of that rabbit's ears. Dara Lynn, of course, threw a fit, and when Ma asked me if I'd done it, I said no. I could feel my cheeks and neck burning red.

"You *sure*, Marty?" she asked. I'd only nodded and left the room. It was one of the worst days of my life.

About an hour later she come out on the porch where I was pushing myself slow in the swing and sat down beside me.

"You know, Marty," she said, "Dara Lynn don't know who ate the ear off her candy rabbit and I don't know who did it, but Jesus knows. And right this very minute Jesus is looking down with the saddest eyes on the person who ate that chocolate. The Bible says that the worst thing that can ever possibly happen to us is to be separated forever from God's love. I hope you'll keep that in mind."

I just swallowed and didn't say anything. But before I went to bed, when Ma asked me again about that rabbit, I gulped and said yes, and she made me get down on my knees and ask God's forgiveness, which wasn't so bad. I honestly felt better afterward. But then she said that Jesus wanted me to go in the next room and tell Dara Lynn what I'd done, and Dara Lynn had a fit all over again. Threw a box of Crayolas at me and could have broke my nose. Called me a rotten, greedy pig. If *that* made Jesus sad, Ma never said.

Now as I study the darkness in the room around me, I'm thinking about lies again. I *hadn't* lied to

56

Judd Travers when I said I hadn't seen his dog in the yard today. That was the honest-to-God truth, because Shiloh hadn't been anywhere near our yard. But I also know that you can lie not only by what you say but what you don't say. Nothing I'd told Judd was an outright lie, but what I'd kept inside myself made him think that I hadn't seen his dog at all.

"Jesus," I whisper finally, "which you want me to do? Be one hundred percent honest and carry that dog back to Judd so that one of your creatures can be kicked and starved all over again, or keep him here and fatten him up to glorify your creation?"

The question seemed to answer itself, and I'm pretty proud of that prayer. Repeat it to myself so's to remember it in case I need to use it again. If Jesus is anything like the story cards from Sunday school make him out to be, he ain't the kind to want a thin, little beagle to be hurt.

The problem's more mixed-up than that, though. Im lying to my folks as well. I'm *not* eating the leftover meat loaf I've put away. Every bit of food saved is money saved that could go to buy Dara Lynn a new pair of sneakers so Ma won't have to cut open the tops of her old ones to give her toes more room. Every little bit of food wasted is money wasted. If we ever have the least little bit of money to spare that doesn't have to go for the care of Grandma Preston, first thing we all want is a telephone so we don't have to ride down to Doc Murphy's to use his. But the way I figure, if it's food from my own plate I would have eaten myself but don't, what's the harm in that?

Next morning when I get up to see Shiloh, I put the rope on his collar and lead him to the other side of the hill again, out of sight of all but God. Then I let him go, and we race and tumble and laugh and roll, stopping now and then just to lie in the clover, me on my back, Shiloh on his stomach, both of us panting and nuzzling each other.

Don't know if Shiloh's gettin' more human or I'm gettin' to be more dog. If Jesus ever comes back to earth again, I'm thinking, he'll come as a dog, because there isn't anything as humble or patient or loving or loyal as the dog I have in my arms right now.

We eat our Sunday meal, but by late afternoon, storm clouds roll in, and the rain beats down on the tin roof of our house, streaming down the window glass, making a small pond in the side yard.

I can't help staring out the window at the far hill. Will Shiloh—*can* he, even—leap that fence to try and go somewhere it's more dry? Is he smart enough to go under that lean-to I'd made for him? Have I built it right, away from the wind? What if he gets to howling?

In twenty minutes the rain stops, though, the sun comes out, the birds start to sing again—all those worms oozing up through the wet mud. Shiloh's stayed where he was, trusting me that where I put him was best. Being quiet, like he knows his life depends on it.

"Marty," Dad says, going outside with a rag to wipe off his Jeep. "I saw Mrs. Howard yesterday and she said David was back from Tennessee, wanting to know when you boys could get together. She said David would like to come up here someday next week."

I like David Howard fine, but I sure don't want him up here. David likes the hill; always wants to play there. He's not afraid of snakes the way Dara Lynn is. David, in fact, likes to go to the very top of that hill and then go running lickety-split down it, racing to see who's first to the fence at the bottom. Likes to climb the trees up there, too, and play lookout.

"Well, I'll go down to David's tomorrow," I say. "I'd rather do that."

"Why not do both?" Ma says, coming out to throw some mash to the hens. "You've hardly seen any friends all summer, Marty. Why don't you go down to Friendly one afternoon and ask David to come up here another?"

"There's nothing much to do up here," I say, not knowing how else to answer.

It was the wrong answer. Both Ma and Dad were looking at me now.

"You said just the other day you had plenty to do here," Dad tells me, wringing out his rag at the pump.

"Lots for me to do, but not much for David Howard," I say. *A lie.* That's a flat-out lie. Funny how one lie leads to another and before you know it, your whole life can be a lie.

I sit on the porch swing later, not even bothering to push it, and listen to the table being set inside.

"What you figure is wrong with that boy, Lou?" Dad's voice.

"Just being eleven, I guess," Ma tells him. "Eleven's a moody age. Was for me, anyways."

"You think that's all it is?"

"What pleases you one day don't please you at all the next. What more do *you* think it is?"

"Don't think he's got that dog on his mind still, do you?"

"Eleven's got about everything on its mind," Ma answers. And then the evening news comes on, and Dara Lynn and Becky come out to the porch, leaving the TV to Daddy.

Dara Lynn's got the devil in her tonight—little

bit bored with summer, but not quite ready for school to start. Just for devilment, she plunks herself down beside me in that swing and starts doin' everything I do. I sigh, she sighs. I rest my arms on my head, she does the same. Gits Becky doin' it, too, both of 'em laughin' to beat the band.

When I have my fill of this nonsense, I decide to go up the hill and see how Shiloh's doin', but as I go down off the porch, Dara Lynn gits up and makes as if to follow me.

I stop. "I'm lookin' to find me a snake stick," I say as if to myself.

"I'm lookin' to find me a snake stick," Dara Lynn says.

I don't pay her no mind at all. Just start walkin' along the edge of the yard, picking up a stick here, a stick there, Dara Lynn tagging along behind.

"It's got to have the longest handle and a good strong fork on the end," I say, "because that was the biggest, meanest snake I ever saw in my life."

Dara Lynn stops dead still. She couldn't say all that right if she tried, but she's not interested anymore in trying. *"What* snake?" she says.

"Snake I saw up on the hill this mornin'," I tell her. "Must have been four, five feet long, just lookin' for somebody's leg to wrap itself around."

Dara Lynn don't go a step farther. Becky don't even come down off the porch.

"What you going to do when you find it?" Dara Lynn asks.

"Try to keep it from bitin' me, first. Pick it up with my stick, second, put it in a sack, and carry it clear on up past the Shiloh schoolhouse, let it out in the woods there. Won't kill it unless I have to."

"Kill it!" says Dara Lynn. "Git your gun and blow its head off."

"You been watchin' too much stuff on TV, Dara Lynn," I tell her. "Even snakes got the right to live." I'm thinking how if I ever become a vet's helper, I got to take care of pet snakes, too.

Next day, to head off David Howard from riding up from Friendly on his bike, I go down to see him. I'd tended to Shiloh first, taking a fistful of scrambled eggs left over from breakfast, a bit of bacon, and a half slice of whole wheat toast that I stuck in my jeans pocket. It's not enough for the dog, I know, but probably more than he'd get from Judd.

It's not enough for me, either. Sneaking off half my breakfast, lunch, and dinner for Shiloh like I'm doing means me going half hungry all the time, but if I eat extra, then it means Shiloh's costing us money we can't afford. I fill my pockets with wormy peaches before I set out for Friendly, biting off each piece, spitting it out in my hand, and picking out the worms before I put it back in my mouth.

It pleased me that Shiloh was sleepin' in his lean-to when I'd gone up that morning. The ground was dry under there, and I'd brought up some old gunnysacks from the shed for him to lie on, made it seem more like a bed to him, more like a home.

The walk to Friendly takes a good long time unless I hitch a ride. I'm not allowed to get in a car with somebody I don't know, but Dad being the mail carrier for this part of the county, I know most everybody who goes by. The first person to come along this day, though, is Judd Travers.

When I hear the sound of a motor and turn to see his truck slowin' down, I turn forward again and keep on walkin', but he pulls up beside me.

"Want a lift?" he sings out.

"No, thanks," I say. "Almost there."

"Where you goin'?"

I couldn't think fast enough to lie. "David Howard's."

"Hell, boy, you ain't even halfway. Hop in."

I know I don't have to unless I want, but if he's already suspicious about me, that'll only make it worse. So I get in.

"See my dog yet?" First thing out of his mouth.

"I been lookin' over all the roads," I tell him in answer. "No beagle."

"Well, I don't think he'd stick to roads," Judd

says. "Not a dog as shy as him. Shy as a field mouse, 'cept when he's around rabbits. That's what the man said who sold him to me, and he sure was right about that."

"How much did you pay for him?" I ask.

"Got him cheap 'cause he's shy. Thirty-five dollars. Worth a lot more'n that as a hunting dog, if I could just keep that damned animal home."

"You got to treat a dog good if you want him to stick around," I say, bold as brass.

"What you know about it?" Judd jerks his head in my direction, then turns the other way and spits his tobacco out the window. "You never even had a dog, did you?"

"I figure a dog's the same as a kid. You don't treat a kid right, he'll run off first chance he gets, too."

Judd laughs. "Well, if that was true, I would have run away when I was four. Far back as I can remember, Pa took the belt to me—big old welts on my back so raw I could hardly pull my shirt on. I stuck around. Didn't have anyplace else to go. I turned out, didn't I?"

"Turned out how?" The boldness in my chest is growing, taking up all the air.

Now Judd sounds mad. "You tryin' to be smart with me, boy?"

"No. Just asking how you turned out, somebody

who was beat since he was four. I feel sorry, is what I feel."

Judd's real quiet a moment. The big old wad of tobacco in his cheek bobs up and down. "Well, don't go wasting your sorry on me," he says. "Nobody ever felt sorry for me, and I never felt sorry for nobody else. Sorry's something I can do without."

I don't say anything at all.

We reach the road where David Howard lives, and the truck slows down.

"I can walk from here," I tell him. "Thanks." I get out.

But as I come around the truck to cross the street, Judd leans out the window. "Like I said, that dog's a shy one. Don't think you'll see much of him near the road, but you keep your eye out for him in the fields. That's where he'll be, more'n likely. You see him, all you got to do is whistle. That's what I teach him. I whistle and he comes to me, he gits fed. But he does somethin' I don't like, I kick him clear to China. You see him, just whistle, then hang on to him and I'll come pick him up. You hear?"

"I hear," I tell him, and keep walking.

CHAPTER 7

David Howard's house is about twice as big as ours for about half as many people. Only him and his ma and dad. Mr. Howard works for the *Tyler Star-News* in Sistersville, and David's ma is a teacher. They're always glad to have me come down to visit, partly because David and I are best friends, and partly, I think, because their old house is so big, the three of 'em get lost in it.

It's got two floors—three counting the basement and four counting the attic. Has four bedrooms upstairs: one for David, one for his folks, one just for company, and one for his father's books, with a computer in it. Downstairs there's a big kitchen, a dining room with a fancy light hanging over the table, a parlor, and a side room with lots of windows just for plants, plus a porch that runs along three sides of the house. I told Ma once the Howards had a room just for company, a room just for books, and a room just for plants, and she said that was three rooms too many. First time I ever saw any envy in my ma.

David says the house used to belong to his great-

granddaddy, so I figure it'll get to be David's someday. Like maybe our little house and the hill and
meadow and the far woods will belong to me and
Shiloh, except I'd probably have to share it with Dara
Lynn and Becky and whoever they marry, and that's
a whole lot of people for four rooms.

"Marty!" Mrs. Howard says when I ring their
doorbell that sounds like church chimes. "We're *so*
glad to see you! Come on in!"

She always means it, too. It's as though she
thinks about me even when I'm not there. Then
David comes whooping downstairs, carrying the helicopter that flies when you pull a string, and pretty
soon we're out in the backyard, chasing around after
the helicopter and telling each other what we've been
doing the six weeks since school let out. I got to bite
my tongue not to let on about Shiloh.

We sit on David's back steps and eat Popsicles
his ma makes out of pineapple juice. I tell David
about the fox I saw with a gray body and a red head,
and he tells me about his aunt's Siamese cat that
yowls just for the pure joy of making noise. Then I
tell him about Judd Travers and how mean he is to
his dogs, not mentioning Shiloh, of course, and then
David says he's got this surprise to show me.

We go upstairs to his room and David says he got
a pet and asks do I want to hold it.

"Sure!" I tell him. "What is it?"

"Sit down and close your eyes and hold out your hands," says David.

I sit down on the edge of his bed and close my eyes and hold out my hands. I expect something warm and wiggly and furry to plop into my arms. Instead I feel something cold and round and plastic, and when I look, it's a fishbowl with sand in it and a hermit crab, scurrying around with a shell on its back. This is a *pet*?

"My first pet!" David says. "His name is Hermie. See all those shells in there? We bought them for him. At night he gets out of one and puts on another, just like changing clothes."

I look at David and I look at that crab in a fishbowl and I want to tell him about Shiloh and how we run up and down the far side of the hill every day and roll in the grass and how he licks my face, but I can't tell him anything. Not yet. Not ever, maybe.

Hermie's sort of fun, though. We get out David's old blocks—the kind you play with back in kindergarten—and we build this big maze with walls on both sides, and then we put Hermie in it. He skids along the maze, looking which way to go, and we laugh when he gets himself in a dead end. I guess any kind of pet's okay once you get used to it, but I wouldn't trade Shiloh for all the hermit crabs in the world.

"When can I come up to your house?" David asks me when we put the blocks away.

"I don't know," I tell him. "Ma's had this sort of headache lately, and she can't take any noise at all." Boy, I am sure asking for trouble with that one.

"We could stay out on that big hill," David suggests. "Chase around in that field. Play lookout."

"Don't think we ought to till she's feeling better," I say. "I'll let you know. But I can come down here again next week, maybe."

I tell Mrs. Howard I got to be home by late afternoon to help out, and she says surely I can stay for lunch, which is what I was hoping. I sit down at the table with place mats, which are little doll-size tablecloths, one under each plate. Mrs. Howard's made us each a chicken-salad sandwich with lettuce and tomato, and toothpicks with olives on top to hold it all together. David's ma is like that. I think it's because she's a teacher—always looking for ways to make something better than it is.

She does the same with boys. She don't just leave us to eat by ourselves. My ma packs us a lunch and lets us eat it out in the woods. Mrs. Howard always sits down to eat with us and talks about grown-up things. Today she tells us about how we've got some new people elected to office who are going to be more honest, she hopes, than the people they defeated, and how the county's going to be better because of it, and so will the whole state of West Virginia. David's ma thinks big.

"You can't just go on electing people to government because they were friends of your father or grandfather," she says, chewing on a bite of celery.

Mostly I'm thinking about the food. I eat every bit of my chicken sandwich. I'm so hungry I don't even save some for Shiloh; then I'm ashamed of myself. Mrs. Howard notices the way I pick up every little crumb, and she says, "I've got enough chicken salad left for another half a sandwich, Marty. Would you like it?"

"Sure would taste good on the walk back home," I tell her, and she sets right to work wrapping it up for me. *Shiloh's dinner*, I tell myself.

But lunch isn't over yet. After the sandwich there's tapioca pudding and chocolate-covered graham crackers, which I love almost as much as Christmas. I don't see any way to get the pudding to Shiloh, so I eat that, but I ask can I take a couple cookies along to eat on the way home, too, and she opens the sack and sticks in six cookies. Ma would have blushed with shame if she heard me ask this, but seems I'm at the point where I'll do most anything for Shiloh. A lie don't seem a lie anymore when it's meant to save a dog, and right and wrong's all mixed up in my head.

Worse than that, when I leave David's house, I
don't even head home. First I go down the street to
the corner store and ask Mr. Wallace does he have any
sort of old cheese or lunch meat he can sell me cheap.
I got fifty-three cents for the cans I collected so far
that Dad turned in for me, and I show Mr. Wallace
how much I got.

"Well, Marty, let me see what I can find back
here," he says, leading me into the little room behind
the counter. He's sort of talking without looking at
me, the way folks do when they don't want to embar-
rass you. "I got some stuff here that's not exactly
spoiled, but it's too old to sell. Wouldn't want your
family getting sick on it, though."

I blush then, 'cause my dad would die of embar-
rassment if he knew what Mr. Wallace is thinking—
that I'm buying this food for our supper, but there's
no way in the world I can let on about Shiloh.

I give him all the change I got, and he lets me
have a big hunk of cheese, moldy on one side, a carton
of sour cream, and half a package of frankfurters that
somebody opened and bought five of. I'm happy as a
flea on a dog. Somehow I know without asking that
Mr. Wallace isn't going to go tellin' folks about it,
because people around here tend to keep quiet out of
someone else's business.

Next problem I got to solve, though, is how to

keep all this stuff from spoiling in the July heat. Can't keep it in our refrigerator or Ma would notice right off. When I get home, Ma's ironing and watching TV and Dara Lynn and Becky's out on the front swing with paper dolls spread out all over the place, so I fish around out in the shed till I find me an old Hi-C can.

I sneak off up the hill with the can and all the food I got with me. Then, with Shiloh watching, I put a rock in the bottom of the can to hold it down, set it in the cool stream, surround it with rocks, and put the container of sour cream, the frankfurters, and the cheese and cookies in there. Put the plastic lid on and set a large rock on top to keep the raccoons out. I'm so proud of myself I like to crow. Hungry again, too, but that half chicken-salad sandwich from Mrs. Howard is Shiloh's dinner, and I give it to him right off.

After that Shiloh and me go on a good long run over the meadow on the far side of the hill, and after I take him back, put fresh water in the pie pan, and love him good, I start down the hill. Halfway to the bottom, here comes Dara Lynn.

"What *you* doin' up here?" I ask her, heart starting to thump.

"Just wanted to see what *you're* doing," she complains. "You go off up here every day almost."

"You leave Becky by herself while Ma's ironing?"

72

"Becky's okay." She turns and follows me back down the hill. Shiloh, up in the pen, don't make a sound. That's how smart a dog he is.

"Well, I was lookin' for that snake again, but he's hiding from me good," I tell her.

"You *still* didn't get him?" she asks, and when I look back, she's got her eyes to the left, then to the right. "You didn't even take your snake stick," she says. *She's* a smart one, too.

"Got me a stick back up on the hill," I tell her.

"How many snakes you figure are up there, Marty?"

"Oh . . . 'bout twenty-nine that you can see. Baby snakes all over the place, though, hiding. Growing into big ones all the time."

Dara Lynn's walking faster now, hurrying to git on by me, watching every place she sets her foot.

I don't feel good about the lies I tell Dara Lynn or David or his ma. But don't feel exactly bad, neither. If what Grandma Preston told me once about heaven and hell is true, and liars go to hell, then I guess that's where I'm headed. But she also told me that only people are allowed in heaven, not animals. And if I was to go to heaven and look down to see Shiloh left below, head on his paws, I'd run away from heaven sure.

CHAPTER 8

Next two days go by smooth as buttermilk. Shiloh gets biscuits or toast and a couple bites of ham for breakfast, and then in the evening, I fix him up some frankfurters, cut up and mixed with sour cream, and little chunks of cheese. He don't much like the cheese. It sticks to his teeth and he turns his head sideways when he chews, trying to get it off. Licks his chops afterward, though.

He throws up the first time he eats the stuff—too rich for his belly, I guess—but after that he manages to keep it down, and all the while he's fattening out a little. Each day it's harder to see his ribs.

I know my secret can't go on forever, though. Only had the dog for six days, and that evening I find out that Judd Travers wants to hunt on our land. Up the hill and over in the far woods. Thinks maybe he could find himself some quail over there, he says.

When Dad tells us that piece of news at dinner, my whole body goes cold. I want to jump up and scream, "No!" but I just grip my chair and wait it out.

"Ray, I don't like that idea at all," Ma says. "You never ask to hunt on his land, and I don't want him hunting on ours. If we let him, we've got to let anyone else who asks, and one of those shots could find its way down here."

"I'll tell him no," Dad says. "Don't like the idea of it myself. I'll tell him the kids play up there."

I stopped gripping the chair, but my heart still goes on thumping hard. I'm thinking how maybe Judd Travers has hold of the idea that I got his dog hid up there and he's looking for an excuse to snoop around. Having Shiloh a secret is like a bomb waiting to go off.

Next day Dad comes home with more news— good news to him, bad news to me.

"Can't figure it out," he says, walkin' through the door with a sack in his hands. "Folks are taking to leavin' me food in their mailboxes, Lou. Used to be it was just Mrs. Ellison and her banana bread, but found me a ham sandwich today in Nora Klingle's box and half a baked pie in the Saunders'. I look thin to you or something?"

Ma laughs. "Maybe it's just you're the best mail carrier they ever had on the route."

"Well, we got half a pie for dessert tonight, anyways," Dad says.

Oh, brother! I say to myself. Maybe Mr. Wallace is doing more talking than I figured. He wouldn't

75

come right out and tell folks I was in his store buying cheap food, but he might just pass it along that the Preston family's in hard times, and suddenly food starts appearing. That's the way it is here.

The next day, Ma rides into town with Dad, taking the girls along, and goes shopping for new sneakers for Dara Lynn and socks and underpants for Becky. First time I have the whole place to myself, and I let Shiloh run pure free. Bring him down the hill to the house, feed him the heels off a loaf of new bread, all the leftover sausage from breakfast, and a bowl of milk. Then I let him lick the oatmeal pan.

Show him every one of our four rooms, hold him in my lap on the porch swing, and laugh when he tries to stand up on the seat himself while the swing's moving. I let him smell the couch where I sleep and crawl under the front steps to sniff out the mole lives under there, follow him all over creation when he takes out after a rabbit. Then he gives up when he sees I'm not going to shoot that rabbit no way.

But I figure my luck's going to run out if I don't get him back to his pen soon, so about noon I take him back, and he goes right to the gunnysacks in the lean-to, he's so tuckered out.

It's just in time, 'cause when I get back and get the dishes done for Ma, the house picked up some, I look out and here she comes up the lane with Dara

Lynn and Becky and their packages. Somebody gave 'em a lift; you can always count on that around Friendly.

Ma's pleased I got the dishes done, I can tell.

"Nice to come back to a clean house, Marty," she tells me. "Had good luck with my shopping, too. Wasn't a thing I bought that wasn't on sale."

Dara Lynn's wore her new sneakers home and got a blister already, but she don't care, she's so glad to have something new.

When I walk in the kitchen next, Ma's looking at her face in the mirror over the sink. Got her eyebrows raised high, then she pushes them low, then raises them again. When she sees me studying her, she says, "Marty, I got frown lines on my face? Tell me the truth now."

I look at her good. "Sure don't see any," I say. I don't neither. Ma's got a pretty face. Plain, but smooth.

"Well, I don't, either, but two people this morning asked me how I was feeling, and one of 'em wants to tell me what to take for headaches. I figure that if folks think I have headaches, I must be doing a lot of frowning."

Whomp, whomp, whomp. That's my heart. "Folks think they got a remedy for something, they'll tell it to you whether you need it or not," I say. Sound so grown-up I hardly recognize myself. So scared inside, though, my stomach's shaking.

Ma's taking out all the things she's bought and putting 'em on the table, taking the price tags off Becky's underpants and socks. "I saw David's mother at the dollar store," she says, "and they've got relatives coming in tonight. She wanted to know if she could bring David up here tomorrow when the rest of them go to Parkersburg. I told her yes."

"Okay," I say, but all the while I'm thinking what I'm going to do with David to keep him off that hill. Take him up toward the old Shiloh schoolhouse, maybe, and walk along the river. Funny thing is, you've got yourself a dog, you sometimes feel like you don't need anyone else. Used to be I'd be waiting at the window for David Howard to come up here for a visit. Nobody else loves you as much as a dog. Except your ma, maybe.

That night Ma makes us fried chicken for supper. First time in a long while. I put away a wing and a thigh on a saucer—to eat later, I tell Ma—and add a spoonful of squash, which might be good for Shiloh's insides. He eats anything. The frankfurters and cheese and sour cream is all gone, so I got to be watching for table scraps again and go out can collecting soon.

Dad's working on the pickup after dinner—

changing the oil—Becky and Dara Lynn's turning somersaults in the grass, and Ma's cleaning the kitchen. Soon as her back is turned, I sneak the food off the saucer and head up the hill to see Shiloh.

I can tell Shiloh likes the fried chicken better than he liked the sour cream-frankfurter mess he'd been eating all week. Even eats the squash, and then he licks my hands and fingers to get all the salt off, anyplace I'd touched a piece of chicken.

Since I'd already taken him all over creation that morning, I don't feel he'll miss much if I don't take him out again, so I go around scooping up all the dog doo, like I do every day, toss it over the fence, and then I lie down on my back in the grass and cover my face with my arms, our favorite game. Shiloh goes nuts trying to uncover my face, nudging at my arms with his nose, tail going ninety miles an hour. Never whines like some dogs do, though. Even when we're out in the far meadow, racing the wind, he'll start to bark and I'll say, "Shhhh, Shiloh!" and he stops right off.

Wish I *could* let him make a little noise. It's not natural, I know, to keep an animal so quiet. But he's *happy*-quiet, not *scared*-quiet. I know that much.

I move my arms off my face after a while and let him rest his paws on my chest, and I'm lying there petting his head and he's got this happy dog-smile

79

on his face. The breeze is blowing cool air in from the west, and I figure I'm about as happy right then as you can get in your whole life.

And then I hear someone say, "Marty." I look up, and there's Ma.

CHAPTER 9

I can't move. Seems as if the sky's swirling around above me, tree branches going every which way. Ma's face even looks different from down on the ground.

Shiloh, of course, goes right over, tail wagging, but all the steam's gone out of me.

"How long have you had this dog up here?" she asks. Not one trace of a smile on her face.

I sit up real slow and swallow. " 'Bout a week, I guess."

"You've had Judd's dog up here a week, and you told him you didn't know where it was?"

"Didn't say I didn't know. He asked had I seen him, and I said I hadn't seen him in our yard. That much was true."

Ma comes around to the trunk of the pine tree, unfastens the wire that holds the fencing closed, and lets herself in. She crouches down in the soft pine needles and Shiloh starts leaping up on her with his front paws, licking at her face.

I can't tell at first how she feels about him, the

way she leans back, away from his dripping tongue. Then I see her hand reach out, with its short, smooth fingers, and stroke him.

"So we've got ourselves a secret," she says at last, and when I hear her say "we," I feel some better. Not a lot, but some.

"How come you to follow me up here tonight?" I want to know.

Now I can tell for sure her eyes are smiling, but her lips are still set. "Well, I had my suspicions before, but it was the squash that did it."

"The squash?"

"Marty, I never.knew you to eat more'n a couple bites of squash in your life, and when you put away a spoonful of that to eat later, I knew for sure it wasn't you doing the eating. And then the way you've been sneaking off every night . . ." She stops stroking Shiloh and turns on me. "I wish you'd told me."

"Figured you'd make me give him back."

"This dog don't belong to you."

"Mine more than Judd's!" I say hotly. "He only paid money for him. I'm the one who loves him."

"That doesn't make him yours. Not in the eyes of the law, it doesn't."

"Well, what kind of law is it, Ma, that lets a man mistreat his dog?"

Ma just sighs then and starts stroking Shiloh's

head. Shiloh wiggles a few inches closer to her on his belly, rests his nose against her thigh, tail going *whick, whack, whick, whack.* Finally Ma says, "Your dad don't know about him?"

I shake my head. More silence. Then she says: "I never kept a secret from your dad in the fourteen years we've been married."

"You ain't going to tell him?"

"Marty, I've got to. He ever finds out about this dog and knows I knew but didn't tell him, how could he trust me? If I keep this one secret from him, he'll think maybe there are more."

"He'll make me give him back to Judd, Ma!" I could hear my voice shaking now. "You *know* he will!"

"What else can we do?"

I can feel hot tears in my eyes now and try to keep them from spilling out. I turn my head till they go away. "Judd Travers ever comes here to get his dog, he'll have to fight me to get it."

"Marty. . . ."

"Listen, Ma, just for one night, promise you won't tell Dad so I can figure out something."

Can tell she's thinking on it. "You aren't fixing to run off with this dog, are you? Marty, don't you *ever* run away from a problem."

I don't answer, because that very thing crossed my mind.

"I can't promise not to tell your dad tonight if you can't promise not to run off."

"I won't run off," I say.

"Then I won't tell him tonight."

"Or in the morning, neither," I add. "I got to have at least one day to think." Don't know what good it will do, though. Have already thought till my brains are dry.

Ma puts out both hands now and scratches behind Shiloh's ears, and he licks her all up and down her arms.

"His name's Shiloh," I tell her, pleased.

After a while Ma gets up. "You coming back to the house now?"

"In a bit," I answer.

It's hard to say how I feel after she leaves. Glad, in a way, that somebody knows: that I don't have to carry this whole secret on my head alone. But more scared than glad. Have me just one day to think of what to do, and not any closer to an answer than I'd been before. I'd spent all my can money on stuff to feed Shiloh. Only money I have now to my name is a nickel I'd found out by the road. Judd won't sell me Shiloh's spit for a nickel.

My first thought is to give him to somebody else and not tell them whose dog it is, then tell Ma that Shiloh had run off. But that would be two more lies to add to the pack. Word would get out some-how or other, and Judd would see David Howard or Mike Wells walking his dog, and then the war would really start.

All I can think of is to take Shiloh down to Friendly the next day, draw me up a big sign that says FREE: WORLD'S BEST DOG or something, and hold it up along the road to Sistersville, hoping that some stranger driving along will get a warm spot in his heart for Shiloh, stop his car, and take him home. And I won't ask him where home is, neither, so when Ma asks me where the dog is, I can tell her honest I don't know.

When I get back to the house, Dad's just wash-ing up at the pump, using grease to get the oil off his arms. He's yelling at Dara Lynn and Becky, who are playing in the doorway, screen wide open, letting in the moths.

I go inside and Ma's putting the dishes away in the kitchen, lifting them out of the drain rack and stacking the plates on the shelf. She's got the radio on and is humming along with a country music song:

> *It's you I wanna come home to,*
> *It's you to bake my bread,*
> *It's you to light my fire,*
> *It's you to share my bed.*

She sort of blushes when she sees me there by the refrigerator, listening to her sing.

I know I'm not going to sleep much that night. I sit on the couch staring at the TV, but not really watching, while Ma gives Becky her bath. Then I wait till Dara Lynn is out of the bathroom so I can take my own bath. Don't know if I soaped up or not. Don't even know if I washed my feet. I go back in the living room, and Ma has my bed made up there on the sofa. The house gets dark, the doors close, and then just the night sounds come from outside.

Know there's a piece of cardboard somewhere out in the shed I can print on. There won't be any trouble getting Shiloh to Friendly, either. I'll put that rope on his collar, and he'll follow along good as anything. We won't take the main road, though, in case Judd's out in his truck. Take every back road I can find.

Then I'll plant myself on the road to Sistersville, holding that sign, Shiloh waiting beside me wondering what it is we're going to do next. What *am* I fixing to do, anyway? Give him to the first car that stops? Don't even know the person driving? Might even be I'll give Shiloh to somebody who'll treat him worse than Judd Travers. Now that Shiloh's come to trust me, here I am getting ready to send him off again. I feel like there's a tank truck sitting on my chest; can't hardly breathe. Got one day to decide what to do with Shiloh, and nothing I think on seems right.

I hear Shiloh making a noise up on the far hill in his pen. Not now, Shiloh! I whisper. You been good as gold all this time. Don't start now. Can it be he knows what I'm fixing to do?

Then I hear a yelp, a loud yelp, then a snarl and a growl, and suddenly the air is filled with yelps, and it's the worst kind of noise you can think of. A dog being hurt.

I leap out of bed, thrust my feet in my sneakers, and with shoelaces flying, I'm racing through the kitchen toward the back door. A light comes on. I can hear Dad's voice saying, "Get a flashlight," but I'm already out on the back porch, then running up the hill.

There are footsteps behind me; Dad's gaining on me. Can hear Shiloh howl like he's being torn in two, and my breath comes shorter and shorter, trying to get there in time.

By the time I reach the pen, Dad's caught up with me, and he's got the flashlight turned toward the noise. The beam searches out the pine tree, the fencing, the lean-to. . . . And then I see this big German shepherd, mean as nails, hunched over Shiloh there on the ground. The shepherd's got blood on his mouth and jaws, and as Dad takes another step

87

forward, it leaps over the fence, same way it got in, and takes off through the woods.

I unfasten the wire next to the pine tree, legs like rubber, hardly holding me up. I kneel down by Shiloh. He's got blood on his side, his ear, a big open gash on one leg, and he don't move. Not an inch.

I bend over, my forehead against him, my hand on his head. He's dead, I know it! I'm screaming inside. Then I feel his body sort of shiver, and his mouth's moving just a little, like he's trying to get his tongue out to lick my hand. And I'm bent over there in the beam of Dad's flashlight, bawling, and I don't even care.

CHAPTER 10

Dad's beside me, holding the flashlight up to Shiloh's eyes. Shiloh's still alive.

"This Judd Travers's dog?"

I sit back on my heels and nod. Wipe one arm across my face.

Dad looks around. "Take those gunnysacks over there and put 'em in the back of the Jeep," he says, and then, still holding the flashlight in one hand, he slips his arms under Shiloh and picks him up. I can see Shiloh wince and pull back on his leg where it hurts.

The tears are spilling out of my eyes, but Dad can't see 'em in the dark. He can probably tell I'm crying, though, 'cause my nose is clogged. "Dad," I say, *"please* don't take him back to Judd! Judd'll take one look at Shiloh and shoot him!"

"Take those gunnysacks to the Jeep like I said," Dad tells me, and I follow behind as we go down the hill. I keep my mouth open to let the breath escape, crying without making a sound. Just like Shiloh.

Ma's watching from inside, the screen all covered with June bugs where they been buzzing about the light. Dara Lynn's up, standing there in her nightshirt, watching.

"What *is* it? What's he got?" Dara Lynn says, pestering Ma's arm.

"A dog," says Ma. And then she calls out, "Ray, is it alive?"

"Just barely," says Dad.

I put the gunnysacks in the Jeep, and Dad carefully lays Shiloh down. Without waiting to ask, I crawl in the Jeep beside Shiloh, and Dad don't say no. He goes in the house for his trousers and his keys, and then we're off.

"I'm sorry, Shiloh," I whisper, over and over, both hands on him so's he won't try to get up. The blood's just pouring from a rip in his ear. "I'm so sorry! Jesus help me, I didn't know Bakers' dog could leap that fence."

When we get to the bottom of the lane, instead of going up the road toward Judd's place, Dad turns left toward Friendly, and halfway around the first curve, he pulls in Doc Murphy's driveway. Light's still on in a window, but I think old doc was in bed, 'cause he come to the door in his pajamas.

"Ray Preston?" he says when he sees Dad.

"I sure am sorry to bother you this hour of the

night," Dad says, "but I got a dog here hurt bad, and if you could take a look at him, see if he can be saved, I'd be much obliged. We'll pay. . . ."

"I'm no vet," says Doc Murphy, but he's already standing aside, holding the screen open with one hand so we can carry Shiloh in.

The doc's a short man, round belly, don't seem to practice what he preaches about eating right, but he's got a kind heart, and he lays out some newspapers on his kitchen table.

I'm shaking so hard I can see my own hands tremble as I keep one on Shiloh's head, the other on a front paw.

"He's sure bleeding good, I can tell you that," Doc Murphy says. He puts on his stethoscope and listens to Shiloh's heart. Then he takes his flashlight and shines it in the dog's eyes, holding each eye open with his finger and thumb. Finally he looks at the big, ugly wound on Shiloh's hurt leg, torn open right to the bone, the bites around Shiloh's neck, and the ripped ear. I turn my head away and sniffle some more.

"I'll do what I can," Doc says. "The thing we got to worry about now is infection. That leg wound is going to take twenty . . . thirty stitches. What happened?"

I figure Dad will answer for me, but he don't—just turns to me. "Marty?"

I swallow. "Big old German shepherd chewed him up."

Doc Murphy goes over to the sink and washes his hands. "Baker's dog? Every time that shepherd gets loose, there's trouble." He comes back to the table and takes a big needle out of his bag, fills it full of something. Something to make Shiloh numb, maybe. "This your dog, son?"

I shake my head.

"No?" He looks at me, then at Dad. Dad still won't say nothing, makes me do the talking. While the doc leans over Shiloh and slowly inserts the needle in his side, I get up my nerve.

"It's Judd Travers's," I tell him. I got to start practicing the truth sometime.

"Judd *Travers's*? This the dog he's missing? How come you brought it in?"

"I had him," I say.

Doc Murphy sucks in his breath, then lets it out a little at a time—*huh, huh, huh.* "Whew!" he says, and goes on about his work.

Don't know how long we're there in Doc's kitchen, Dad standing over against the wall, arms folded, me with my hands cupped over Shiloh's head while Doc Murphy washes the wounds, dresses them, and starts stitching the skin back up. Once or twice I feel Shiloh jerk, like it hurts him, but when he lays too still, I don't know if it's because he's numb or if he's dying.

"The next twenty-four hours, we'll know if this dog's going to live," the doc says. "You check with me tomorrow evening; we'll have some idea then. I can keep him here for a day or two, Ray. Then, if he makes it, you can take him on home."

I put my face down near Shiloh's again, my mouth next to his ear. *"Live,* Shiloh, *live!"* I whisper.

Hardest thing in the world is to leave Shiloh there at Doc Murphy's, the way his eyes follow me over to the doorway, the way his muscles move, like he's trying to get up when he sees me leaving. Second hardest thing is to crawl in the Jeep with Dad afterward.

There isn't a word passed between us till we get home. Once Dad turns the motor off, though, and I'm all set to get out, he says, "Marty, what else don't I know?"

"What?" I ask.

"You keeping Judd's dog up there on our hill— got a place for him all built, never letting on. What else you keeping from me?"

"Nothing, Dad!"

"How do I know that's not another lie?"

" 'Cause it's not."

"You saying so don't make it true."

93

I know then what Ma meant. But it's not all so black and white as Dad makes it out to be, neither. And sometimes, when I get mad, it clears my head.

"You would have thought more of me if I'd let that dog wander around till Judd found it again, kick the daylights out of 'im?" I ask. "That what you want me to do, Dad?"

"I want you to do what's right."

"What's right?"

For once in my eleven years, I think I have my dad stumped. Leastways, it seems to be thirty . . . forty seconds before he answers:

"You've got to go by the law. The law says a man that pays money for a dog owns that dog. You don't agree with the law, then you work to change it."

"What if there isn't time, Dad? Shiloh could be dead by the time somebody looked into the way Judd treats his dogs."

Dad's voice is sharp: "You think Judd Travers is the only one around here hard-hearted toward his animals? You think he's the only one who starves 'em or kicks 'em or worse? Open up your eyes, Marty. *Open your eyes!*" Now Dad half turns in his seat, back resting against the door, facing me: "How many times have you walked to the school bus and seen a chained-up dog in somebody's yard? How many times you ever put your mind to whether or not it's happy, its ribs sticking out like handles on the sides?

94

Suddenly you're face-to-face with a dog that pulls at your heart, and you all at once want to change things."

I swallow. "There's got to be a first time," I answer.

Dad sighs. "You're right about that," he says.

I'm pushing my luck, I know. "If Doc Murphy don't tell Judd about Shiloh, can we bring him back here and keep him? I could build him a better pen. Make the fence high enough so the shepherd can't get in."

Dad opens the Jeep door on his side. "No," he says, and gets out.

I get out, too. "Just till Shiloh's better, then? You know how Judd treats anything that don't work right. He'll shoot Shiloh, Dad! I found a dog once before over near Judd's place with a bullet hole in his head. We could at least get Shiloh well. I'm going to pay Doc Murphy's bill. I promise you that. You get all my can money for the next three years, and I'll deliver the county paper, too, if I get the chance. Honest! I promise!"

Dad studies me. "You can keep him here till he's well, that's all. Then we're taking him back to Judd." And he goes in the house.

My heart starts pounding again. *Thumpity, thump. Thumpity thump.* There's still time, I'm thinking. Shiloh's still alive, and I ain't licked yet.

CHAPTER 11

It's only after I lie back down on the couch that night that I realize what all I've done. To Ma and Dad, for one thing. Ma's still awake. I can see the light in the bedroom as Dad goes on down the hall. And then I hear their voices. Not all of what they say, but enough:

"Ray . . . told you I just found out about that dog myself. . . ."

". . . secrets from me, you and Marty."

". . . till tomorrow. I would have told you then. . . ."

". . . every day . . . the mail to Judd's place . . . mentions that dog to me, and all the time . . . up on my own property, me not even knowing. . . ."

I bring my arms up against my ears and hold 'em there. So many things going wrong, it's hard to remember anything going right. Doc Murphy knows I've got Judd's dog now, Dad's mad at Ma, and we won't know till tomorrow if Shiloh's even going to make it. Worst of all, I'd brought Shiloh here to keep him from being hurt, and what that German shepherd done to him was probably worse than anything Judd Travers would have brought himself to do, short of shootin' him, anyways. This time, when the tears come again, I don't even fight. Don't even try holding back.

I must have slept through Dad's going off to work the next morning, 'cause when I wake, Becky's standing beside the couch eating a piece of honey toast and breathing on my face. Dara Lynn's already told her about the dog, because she asks right off, "Where's it at, the doggy?"

I sit up and tell her the dog's at Doc Murphy's and we'll find out how he is that afternoon. Then I look in the kitchen at Ma. There's the set look about the lips that means trouble—that means don't mess with her, 'cause she's already in trouble with Dad.

I go outside, pick me a couple wormy peaches, and sit on the stoop, eating at them, spitting out the wormy places.

Dara Lynn comes out and sits beside me. Today she's all kindness.

"Judd Travers don't take care of his dog, Marty, no wonder it come up here," she says, trying to say the right thing. I can tell she's been figuring it all out, from what she could overhear between Ma and Dad and anything else Ma told her.

I take another bite of peach.

"It wasn't like you *stole* him," she says. "That dog come up here on its own."

"Just hush up, Dara Lynn," I say, which I had no business saying. I didn't want to talk to anyone, that's all.

"Well, you could have told me and I wouldn't have told anyone."

"Thanks."

"Ma says we've got to give him back to Judd Travers when he's better."

I get up and start toward the hill to clean up the ground where Shiloh was attacked. See if there's any way I can put some fence wire over the top of the pen to keep out the shepherd.

"What's his name, Marty?" Dara Lynn calls after me.

"Shiloh," I tell her.

I'm only halfway up the hill when I hear a car and turn around. It's Mrs. Howard's car, and David's in it. Soon as he sees me he jumps out—it still moving a little—and comes running toward me.

"I get to stay here today!" he yells, waving a kite he's brought with him. "Everyone else is going to Parkersburg and I didn't want to go."

I look over to where Ma and Mrs. Howard are talking, see Ma nodding her head. I get lonely sometimes up at our house, but today I want to be with that loneliness. Don't want to talk to Dara Lynn, to Becky, to Dad, or even to Ma. If we had a telephone, I'd be calling Doc Murphy every hour. As it is, I have to wait till Dad comes home from work before I can find out about Shiloh. Can't go down there pesterin' Doc, him with patients to see.

"What do you want to do?" I ask David, trying to dig up the least little bit of enthusiasm. David and I are in the same grade, even though he's taller and heavier and looks like junior high already.

"Try out this kite over in your meadow," he says.

I lead him around the long way, away from Shiloh's pen, and he doesn't even notice because he's unwrapping his kite, made of silk or something, which one of his relatives brought him.

We stand out in the meadow flying the kite, and I watch the blue-and-yellow-and-green tail whipping around in the breeze, and I'm thinking about Shiloh's tail, the way it wags. You get a dog on your mind, it seems to fill up the whole space. Everything you do reminds you of that dog.

When we bring the kite down later, though, David sees a groundhog, and next thing you know he's after it—the groundhog zigzagging this way and that, David yelling like crazy.

"I'm taking your kite back down to the house, David," I yell when I see him getting near Shiloh's pen.

He goes on running and yelling.

"I'm going to get me a handful of soda crackers. You want to make some peanut-butter-cracker sandwiches?" I call out, trying to get him to follow.

And then his yelling stops. "Hey!" he says.

I know he's found the pen, and I walk over.

"What's this?" David asks. He looks at the blood on the ground. "Hey! What happened here?"

I go over and yank his arm and make him sit down. He's looking at me bug-eyed.

"You listen to me, David Howard," I say. Whenever I say "David Howard," he knows it's serious. Only did it twice in my life—once when he sat on the paper flowerpot I'd made for Ma at school, and once when he saw me with my pants down in the bathroom. That really made me mad.

But today I'm not mad, I'm serious: "Something awful and terrible happened in there, David, and if you ever tell anyone, even your ma and dad, may Jesus make you blind."

That's the kind of talk my folks can't stand, but I got it from Grandma Preston herself. Ma says Jesus don't go around making anyone blind, but Grandma Preston always used it as a warning and she went to church Sunday morning and evening both.

David's eyes about to pop out of his head. *"What?"* he asks again.

"You know Judd Travers?"

"He was *murdered*?"

"No. But you know the way he's mean to his dogs?"

"He killed one of his dogs in there?"

"No. Let me *tell* it, David. You know how he's missing a dog?"

"Yeah?"

"Well, it come up here on its own and I let him stay. I built him a pen and kept him secret and named him Shiloh."

David stares at me, then at the blood in the pen, then back at me again.

"Last night," I tell him, "Bakers' German shepherd jumped the fence and tore him up. We took Shiloh to Doc Murphy, and Judd don't know."

David's mouth falls open and hangs there. "Wow!" he says, then says it again.

I tell David how hurt Shiloh was and how we've got to wait till tonight to see how he is, and then we go in his pen together, and David helps me clean up the blood—pull up all the grass with blood stains on it and throw it over the fence into the woods.

It's easier somehow with David helping. With David knowing, even. If it was me by myself, I'd be thinking again and again how this never would have happened if Shiloh could have got away from the shepherd. I look at David and think we're friends for life. Then I think of how there are exactly seven people now who know I have Judd Travers's dog, and it's only a matter of time before somebody lets it out. Probably Becky. She'll warble it to the first person coming up the lane. Did you ever notice how the more a little kid tries not to tell a secret, the sooner it gets out? Nothing that child can do about it. A secret is just too big for a little kid.

What I didn't expect was that at three-thirty, before Dad come home, here's Doc Murphy's car chugging up the lane, and he's got Shiloh in the backseat. I'm standing out by the oak tree with David, taking turns on the bag swing, when I see the car and Shiloh's head raised up in the backseat. I'm over to that car in three seconds flat.

"Shiloh!"

No cry ever sounded so happy as the one that come up out of my throat.

All of us, we're crowding around the car—Ma and Dara Lynn and Becky and David Howard, and all of us are saying, "Shiloh! Here, boy!" and holding out our hands, and Shiloh's trying to lick everything in sight.

"Patient recovered faster than I thought he would," Doc says, getting his big belly out from behind the steering wheel and standing up. "So I figured I'd bring him on over myself." And then, to Mother, "Had patients coming in and out today, and don't know that I wanted them to see the dog."

She nodded.

"I'm going to pay for this, Doc Murphy," I tell him. "You send the bill to Dad and he'll pay it, but then I'm payin' him."

"Well, son, that's a generous thing to do, with a dog not even yours," he says.

"Is he all well now?"

"No. Not by a long shot. Think it's going to take a couple weeks to heal, and I can't promise you he'll walk without a limp. But I got him sewn back up and full of antibiotics. If you can keep him quiet for a few days and off that leg, I think he'll pull through just fine."

If Ma was mad at me before, she's not now, not the way Shiloh's licking her all over both arms, getting a quick lick in at her face every time she bends close. Becky's sticking her hand out for Shiloh to lick, and when he does, she squeals and pulls back. Shiloh's tail going like crazy.

It's like a welcome-home party. Ma has me bring in this cardboard box from the shed and we put an old pillow in the bottom of it and cover it with a clean sheet, and Doc Murphy lays Shiloh down inside it.

SHILOH

Shiloh seems to know he can't walk too good, because as soon as he tries to stand up, he sits back down again and licks at his leg.

I'm glad Shiloh's back, I'm glad he's going to get better, and that we can keep him till he's well. But the more I sit there petting his head, feeling his happiness, the more I know I can't give him up. I won't.

CHAPTER 12

Sure seems strange having Shiloh in the house that night, after trying so hard to keep him secret. Strange, too, the way Ma takes to him. Seems like she can't hardly pass his box next to the stove without reaching down to pet him, making low sympathy noises in her throat, way she does when Dara Lynn or Becky or me gets sick.

Dad don't say much. He come home to find Shiloh there, he just stands off to one side, listening to what Doc Murphy said about him; he don't get close enough for Shiloh to take a lick.

But when supper's over and I go off to the bathroom to brush my teeth, I peek back through the doorway, and Dad's over by Shiloh's box, letting him lick his plate clean. Dad crouches there a minute or two, scratching all down Shiloh's back and up again.

What I'm figuring, see, is by the time Shiloh's better, everybody will love him so much they just can't let him go—even Dad. I'm hoping Dad will go over to see Judd Travers, make him an offer for

Shiloh, and then he'll be ours. The trouble with this kind of thinking, though, is we don't have the money.

I'll probably be through junior high school, almost, before I earn enough to pay Doc Murphy's bill. To buy Shiloh from Judd, even if Judd's willing to sell, I'd have to collect aluminum cans all through high school, too. Can't make very much with cans. I try to think about what other kind of work I can do that would pay me more, but except for delivering the county paper on Friday afternoons, nothing else comes to mind. And somebody's got that job already.

It's sort of like Shiloh's there and he's not. In the next couple of days, everybody's pettin' him every chance they get. Becky feeds him the crusts off her toast—breaks off little bits, and shrieks every time she feels Shiloh's mouth slurp them out of her fingers.

Ma's putting up beans in jars, and all the while she hums to Shiloh like he's a baby in a cradle, not a dog in a box. Dara Lynn's got an old hairbrush, and she just can't seem to brush that dog enough. Even Dad sits down one evening and gets out every tick Shiloh's got on him. Takes a little dab of turpentine and rubs it on the tick's rear end, and the tick backs out of Shiloh's skin mighty quick.

The thing that makes it seem like Shiloh's *not* there is that nobody except me and Dara Lynn and

Becky talks about him. Ma and Dad don't even once mention his name out loud, as though saying it makes him ours, which he ain't. As though if you don't talk about him, maybe he'll disappear as quietly as he come that day in the rain.

What everyone's waiting for, I guess, is something to happen. Every day Shiloh's getting a little stronger. Two days after Doc Murphy brought him here, Shiloh's up limping around on his bad leg. Ma puts some papers beside his box for him to do his business on, but he won't, so for the first couple days I pick him up, carry him out to the yard, and after he's done his business there, I bring him in again. But now he's pushing open the back screen himself and going down into the yard, then comin' back and tapping on the screen with one paw, so we'll let him in. Somebody, sometime, is bound to see him. Becky, sometime, bound to say something. Even David Howard, when his ma came to pick him up the other day, opens his mouth right off and says something about Shiloh.

"Who's Shiloh?" she asks, and David realizes he's let it slip.

"Old stray cat," he says, and now I've got David lying.

Worse part about having Shiloh here in the house where I can play with him anytime I like is that it's hard to leave him when I go out collecting cans. But I've got to earn money now more than ever, so each day, when Shiloh takes his long nap, I set out with my plastic garbage bag hanging out one jeans' pocket.

One day I walk all the way to Friendly and ask at the grocery, where the county paper is dropped, if they'll put in my name as a carrier. Mr. Wallace says he'll turn my name in, but he's already got six names ahead of me, and one of 'em is a grown man with a car. Don't see how I can match that.

I study the bulletin board at the back of the store where people put up notices. Stand on one foot and then the other reading the whole danged board, and seems like everybody got something to sell, or want to be hired, nobody wants to buy. Only two jobs listed, one for an appliance salesman and some woman who wants her house painted.

Mr. Wallace sees me looking at the board, and he comes over and takes down the notice about a woman wanting her house painted.

"That's already taken," he tells me.

That night, while we finish supper, Shiloh's going around the table, putting his nose in everyone's lap, looking mournful, waiting for somebody to slip him something to eat. I can tell Ma and Dad's trying their best not to laugh. Ma won't let us feed him at the table.

What I'm dying to ask Dad is did he tell Judd Travers about his dog being here. Dad don't mention it so I don't ask. Maybe I don't want to know, I tell myself.

And then, just as Ma's dishing up a peach cobbler that we're going to eat hot with milk, I hear a sound outside that makes my bones feel like icicles inside me.

Shiloh hears it, too, and I know right away it's what I think it is, because Shiloh sticks his tail between his legs, puts his belly low to the floor, and climbs back into his box.

Ma and Dad look at Shiloh. They look at each other. Then there's the slam of a truck door outside, footsteps on the ground, footsteps on the porch, and a *rap, rap, rap* at the back door. Everybody stops eating, like we was all froze to death in our chairs.

Dad gets up and turns on the porch light, and there he is, Judd Travers, looking as mean and nasty as I ever seen him look. He don't even ask can he come in; just opens the screen and steps inside.

"Ray Preston," he says, "somebody told me you got my dog."

Dad's looking serious. He nods and points toward the box by the stove. "Over there, Judd, but he's hurt, and we've been taking care of him for you."

Judd stares at Shiloh and then at Dad. "Well, I'll

be danged," he says, almost softly. "Somebody knows my dog is missing, takes him in, and don't even have the decency to tell me?"

"We *were* going to tell you," Dad says, and he's looking straight at Judd. "Nobody wants to hear his dog's been hurt, though, and we wanted to make sure he was going to pull through." Then he turns to me. "Marty," he says, "you want to tell Mr. Travers how his dog come to be here?"

He knows I don't. He knows I'd rather swim a river full of crocodiles than face Judd Travers. But it's my story to tell, not Dad's, and he always did make us face up to what we'd done.

"Your dog come over here twice because you been mistreatin' it," I say, and my voice don't sound near as strong as Dad's. Sort of quavery. I clear my throat and go on: "So second time it come over, I built it a pen up in the woods and Dad didn't know it, and that German shepherd of Baker's got in and fought Shiloh."

"Fought who?"

"The beagle. Shiloh, that's what I've been callin' him. And Shiloh got hurt bad. It was my fault for not making the fence higher. We took him to Doc Murphy and he patched him up."

Judd Travers is still staring around the room like he never saw the likes of us before. Finally he lets out his breath through his teeth and slowly shakes his head: "And I got to find out all this from Doc Murphy?"

I couldn't believe Doc would go tell him.

"Somebody goes to the doc the other day and sees a beagle lying out on his back porch. Tells me about it later. Says he thinks maybe the dog's mine. So I ride over to Doc's this evening, and he tells me it was you who brought him in."

Judd walks across the kitchen, and at the thud of each footstep, Shiloh huddles down farther and farther in the box, like maybe he can make himself disappear. His whole body is shaking. Ma sees it, I know, because she watches for a minute, then turns her face away quick.

Judd stares down at Shiloh—at his bandage and the shaved place where he's all stitched up—the rip on his ear. "Look what you done to my *dog*!" he yells at me, eyes big and angry. I swallow. Nothin' I can say to that.

Travers squats down by the box. He puts out his hand, and Shiloh leans away, like he's going to be hit. If that don't prove the way he treats 'em, I don't know what would, but Judd's saying, "I never mistreated my dogs. This one was shy when I got him, that's all. I sure never caused him an injury like this one. Wouldn't never have happened if you'd brought him back like I told you." I close my eyes.

When I open 'em again, Judd's putting his hand

111

on Shiloh's head, roughlike, sort of patting him, and you can tell he ain't got that much practice being kind. Still, hard to prove Shiloh wasn't mistreated *before* he got to Judd's. How do you go about proving something like that?

"It was wrong of Marty to pen up your dog, Judd, and we've already talked about that," Dad says. "He's the one who's going to pay Doc Murphy for patching him up, and soon as the dog is strong, we'll drive him over to your place. Why don't you let us keep him until then, in case he needs more care?"

Judd stands up again and looks at me. I stare back, but I don't say nothing.

And then Ma can't take it anymore. She says, "Judd, Marty's got awful attached to that dog, and we'd like to know how much you want for it. Maybe we can scrape up the money to buy him."

Judd looks at her like she's talking some kind of nonsense, like we are all getting crazier by the minute.

"That dog's not for sale," he says. "Paid good money to get me a hunting dog, and he could be one of the best I've had. You want to keep and feed him till he's better, okay with me. It's you that got him all tore up, and you paying the bill. But I want him back by Sunday."

Screen door slams again, truck starts up, and then he's gone.

CHAPTER 13

I'm back to not sleeping again. Everything I can think of to try, I've already thought on and turned down. Even thought of Dad and me driving to Middlebourne and going to the county courthouse to report a man who's mean to his dogs, thinking maybe they wouldn't let Judd have Shiloh back again. Dad says that's where we'd have to go, all right, but how am I going to prove it about Judd? Think about that, he says.

I been thinking about it. Do I really suppose they'd send an investigator all the way out from Middlebourne to see about a man said to kick his dogs? And if they did, do I think Judd's going to tell the man yes, indeed, he does kick them? Do I think the investigator's going to hide out in the bushes near Judd Travers's place for a week just to see for himself?

Tyler County hasn't hardly got the money to investigate reports of children being kicked, Dad says, much less dogs. Even if I told the animal-rights people that I found a dog with a bullet hole in its head up near Judd's house, don't prove that Judd was the one who killed it.

I go out to talk to Dad about it some more while he's chopping wood, and he just says, "Son, it's hard, I know, but sometimes you just got to do what has to be done. It's Judd's dog and there's no getting around it."

Ma tries to make me feel better. She says at least I brought some joy and kindness into the life of a dog that never had any before, and that Shiloh will never forget me. But that even makes it worse. Wish he *could* forget. Keep thinking of how Shiloh's going to look at me when we drive him over to Judd's, and my eyes fill up again. Becky, she's been crying, too. So has Dara Lynn. The one good thing about it now is that the whole family loves Shiloh and we can talk about him out loud, but there's not one thing we can do. Three more days and we have to give him up.

I walk down to Friendly on Friday to talk with David Howard. David feels almost as bad as I do. I hardly finish telling about Shiloh and he's got tears in his eyes already. David Howard's thirty pounds heavier and bigger than me, and he still don't care who sees him cry.

"I been thinking, David," I say. "You got relatives in Ohio, don't you?"

He nods.

"You think any of them would take Shiloh?

Could you call 'em up and ask could they drive down here tomorrow and take him back with them, and I'll tell Judd we let Shiloh out one day and he never come back?" More lies.

But David's shaking his head already. "It's only Uncle Clyde and Aunt Pat, and she's allergic to dogs. They had one once and had to give him up."

On the way back home, I'm thinking about someplace really good I could hide that dog. The old gristmill, maybe, up by the bridge. The door's padlocked, but it don't take much to get in, 'cause the top of the building's open where some of the roof's blown away. I bet I could hide Shiloh in there for ten years and he'd never make a sound. But what kind of life is that? Couldn't never take him anywhere except after dark. Even then, he'd be so close to Judd's place, the other dogs would probably sniff him out.

Slowly the minutes and hours of Friday tick by, then it's Saturday, and our last day with Shiloh. We give him every little treat we can think of, a wonder we don't make him sick, and after supper we sit out on the back porch like we usually do. Becky and Dara Lynn are rolling around in the grass, and Shiloh limps out there to join in the fun. I show Becky how if you lay down on your stomach with your arms up over your face, Shiloh will work to turn you over. Both girls have to try it, and Shiloh does just like I said, trying his best to get those girls up on their feet.

"If Becky ever fell in the creek, I'll bet Shiloh would pull her out," Ma says.

"If I ever saw a snake, I'll bet Shiloh would kill it for me," says Dara Lynn.

I got a sadness inside me growing so big I feel I'm about to bust. That night I sleep a little bit, wake a bit, sleep a bit, wake some more. About dawn, however, I know what I got to do.

I get up quiet as can be. Soon as Shiloh hears me, of course, he's out of his box.

"Shhh, Shiloh," I say, my finger to my lips. He watches me a moment, then crawls back in his box, good as ever.

I dress, pull on my sneakers, take me a slice of bread from the loaf on the counter and a peach off the tree in the yard. Then I take the shortcut through the east woods toward Judd Travers's.

It's the only thing left to do. I'd talked to Dad, to Ma, to David, and nobody's got any more idea what to do than they did before. What I'm fixing to do is talk to Judd Travers straight and tell him I'm not going to give Shiloh back.

Rehearsed my lines so often I can say 'em by heart. What I don't know, though, is what Judd's going to say—what he's going to do. I'll tell him he can beat me, punch me, kick me, but I'm not going to give that dog up. I'll buy Shiloh from Judd, but if he won't sell and comes to get him, I'll take Shiloh and head out in the other direction. Only way he can get his dog back is to take me to court, and then I'll tell the judge how Judd treats his animals.

Halfway through the woods, I'm thinking that what I'm about to do could get my dad in a whole lot of trouble. Around here it's serious business when you got a quarrel with your neighbor and you got to carry it as far as the law. Folks ain't that fond of Judd, and most of 'em likes my dad, but when it comes to taking a man's property, I figure they'll side with Judd. I'm not makin' life one bit easier for my parents or Dara Lynn or Becky, but I just can't give up Shiloh without a fight.

Will he shoot me? That thought crosses my mind, too. Some kid got shot down in Mingo County once. Easy as pie for Judd Travers to put a bullet hole in my head, say he didn't see me. I got my feet pointed toward Judd Travers's place, though, and they ain't about to turn back.

Still so early in the morning the mist is rising up out of the ground, and when I come to a stretch of field, looks like the grass is steaming. Sky's light, but the sun hasn't showed itself yet. You live in hill country, it takes a while for the sun to rise. Got to scale the mountains first.

SHILOH

I'm practicing being quiet. What I hope is to get to Judd's house before he's wide awake, take him by surprise. He sees me coming a half mile off, without Shiloh, he's likely to figure what I got to say and have his answer ready. I want to be sitting there on his porch the moment he gets out of bed.

A rabbit goes lickety-split in front of me, then disappears. I went out hunting with Dad once, and he said that when you first scare up a rabbit, it hops a short way, then stops and looks back. That's when you got to freeze. Can't move nothing but your eyeballs, Dad says. What you have to look for is that shiny black dot—the rabbit's eye. If you look for the whole rabbit, you almost never see him because he blends into the scenery.

So I don't move a muscle and look for the shiny black dot. And there it is. I wonder what's going on inside that rabbit—if its heart's pounding fierce. No way I could tell it I wasn't going to do it harm. So I go on, back into the second stretch of woods, heading for that second field.

I'm just about to come out of the trees when I stop dead still again, for right there in the meadow is a deer, a young doe. She's munching on something, and every so often she stops, looks up, then goes on eating again.

Hardest thing in the world for me to see how

118

anybody could shoot an animal like that. Then I
think of a couple winters ago we hardly had any meat
on our table, and I guess I can see how a father with
three kids could shoot a deer. Hope I never have to,
though. I'm just about to step out into the meadow,
when *crack!*

It's the sound of a rifle. It splits the air and
echoes back against the hills.

The doe takes out across the meadow, heading
for the woods. Its front legs rear up, then its back legs
as it leaps, its tail a flash of white.

Crack!

The rifle sounds again, and this time the deer
goes down.

I can't move. One part of me wants to go to the
deer, the other part knows that somebody's out here
with a rifle shooting deer out of season. And before
I can decide whether to go on or turn back, out of
the woods on the other side steps Judd Travers, rifle
in hand.

CHAPTER 14

He's wearing this army camouflage shirt, a brown cap, and the weirdest grin that could fit on a human face.

"Whooeee!" he says, holding the rifle up with one hand as he plows through the weeds. "I got 'er! Whooeee!"

I know he wasn't out shooting rabbits and happened to get a doe instead, because he doesn't have his hounds with him; Judd Travers had gone out that morning with the clear intention of getting himself a deer. I also know that if the game warden finds out about it, Judd's in big trouble, 'cause the deer he shot out of season wasn't even a buck.

He slogs over through waist-high weeds to where the doe lays. Bending over, he looks at her, walks around her a little piece, then says "Whooeee!" again, soft-like.

That's when I come out of the woods. He's got his back to me now, his hands on the doe's front legs, trying to see can he pull her himself. Drags her a little way and stops. And when he looks up again, I'm right beside him.

He whirls around. "Where'd you come from?" he says.

"Was on my way over to see you," I tell him, and for the first time, standing next to Judd Travers, I feel taller than I really am.

He looks at me a moment like he don't know if he's glad I'm there or not. Then I guess he figures me being there, only a kid, don't matter. "Look what I got!" he says. "Found her eatin' at my garden this morning, and I chased her over here."

"That's a lie," I say. "I was back in the woods watching her eat. She was comin' down from the hills the other way. You went out deer huntin' for anything you could get."

"Well, supposing I did!" says Judd Travers, and he hates me worse'n snot.

"Deer ain't in season, that's what," I answer. "There's a two-hundred-dollar fine for killing a doe."

Judd Travers is staring at me like he's about to crack me across the mouth. Way we're raised around here, children don't talk back to grown folks. Don't hardly talk much at all, in fact. Learn to listen, keep your mouth shut, let the grown folks do the talking. And here I am, shooting off my mouth at five-thirty in the morning to a man holding a rifle. Am I crazy or what?

"Not unless the game warden finds out, there's not," Judd says. "And who's going to tell him? You?"

All at once I realize I got Judd Travers right where I want him. One way you look at it, it's my duty to report a killed doe. The way folks up here look at it, though, that's snitching. And if I *might* could tell, but bargain not to, it's something else again: It's blackmail. But, like I said, I'd got to the place I'd do most anything to save Shiloh.

"Yeah," I say, my heart pounding like crazy. "I'll tell. There's a free number to call." There is, too. It's on Dad's hunting regulation papers. Boy, I sure didn't know I was going to step into all this when I come up here this morning.

Now Judd's looking at me good, eyes narrowed down to little slits. "Your pa put you up to this?"

"No. This is me talking."

"Well, ain't you something now! And who's to believe you?"

"I'll get the game warden up here, show him the spot the doe was hit, the blood, and when he finds the deer at your place, he'll believe me." The words are coming out quicker than I can think, almost.

"I'll tell him he was eatin' my garden."

"And I'll say different. The new game warden won't make any allowance even if the deer *was* eating your garden. You just don't shoot deer out of season no way. 'Specially a doe."

Now Judd's really angry, and his words come at me like bees. "What you trying to do, boy? Start up trouble? You think I can't put you in your place mighty quick?"

"So what you going to do?" I ask. "Shoot me?"

Travers is so surprised his jaw drops. But I'm cooking now. Nothing can stop me. Braver than I ever been in my life.

"Going to shoot me like that dog I found up here six months back with a bullet in his head?"

Travers stares some more.

"I know whose bullet that was, Judd, and I told Dad, and if folks find me up here with a bullet in me, Dad'll know whose bullet that is, too."

I can't hardly believe the words that's coming out of my mouth. Been scared most my life of Judd Travers, and here I am, half his size, talking like a grown person. It's because I know Shiloh's still got a chance.

"So what you waiting for?" Judd says finally. "Go get the game warden." And when I don't move, he says, "Come off it, Marty. Here. You take one of those legs, I'll take another, we'll drag it to my place, and I'll give you half the meat. And don't tell me your ma won't be glad to get it."

"I don't want the meat. I want Shiloh."

Now Judd's really surprised and whistles through his teeth. "Boy, you just come up here to set me up, didn't you?"

"Didn't have an idea in this world you was out with your rifle," I tell him, and that's one of the first truths I told in two weeks. "I come up here because it's Sunday, the day you said to bring your dog back, and I wanted you to know you got to fight me first to get him. Now I'm telling you I mean to keep him, and you expect to keep that deer without a fine, you'll make the trade."

"Whoa!" says Travers. "That's no kind of trade at all! If I *hadn't* got me a deer this morning, what would you have bargained with then?"

I didn't have an answer to that because I hadn't been thinking about a deal. Judd had already said he wouldn't sell Shiloh.

Judd's eyes narrow down even more till it almost looks like he's asleep. "I just bet you *would* tell the game warden, too."

"Jesus' name, I would."

"And you're sayin' if I let you keep my huntin' dog, you're going to keep this deer a secret?"

I begin to see now I'm no better than Judd Travers—willing to look the other way to get something I want. But the something is Shiloh.

"Yes, I will," I tell him, not feeling all that great about it.

"Well, you got to do more than that, boy, because I paid thirty-five dollars for that dog, and I want forty to let him go."

For the first time, I see a thin ray of hope that maybe he'll let me buy Shiloh. "I'll get you the money somehow, by and by," I promise.

"I don't want the money by and by. I want it now. And you haven't got it now, you work for me and pay it off."

You make a deal with Judd Travers and you're only eleven years old, you take what you can get. But all I'm thinking is *dog.*

"You got a bargain," I tell Judd, and now my feet want to dance, my face wants to smile, but I don't dare let the delight show through.

"You listen here," says Judd. "I'll pay you two dollars an hour, and that comes to twenty hours to earn forty dollars. And the work ain't easy."

"I'll do it," I say.

"Beginning now," says Judd, and I can tell he's gettin' a bit edgy that someone else might come through the field, wondering about those rifle shots, and see how he got a doe. "Help me get this deer to my trailer."

I'm so glad to be gettin' Shiloh, I can hardly think straight. But I'm thinkin' straight enough as I help drag that doe to Judd's to know that by lettin' him get away with this, I'm putting other deer in danger. He kill this one out of season, he'll figure maybe he can kill some more. To save Shiloh, I'm making it harder for deer. I swallow. All I got to do, though, is think of the way he'd look at me, I ever give him back to Judd, and then I get on with my job.

When we get to the trailer at last, we carry the deer around to the three-sided shed Judd's got in his backyard. First thing Judd does is bleed the doe, keep the meat from spoilin'. Then he goes out and messes up the tracks with his foot, kicking up the grass where we'd matted it down, and covering the trail of blood with dust.

"I git home from work every day at three," Judd says, "and I want you here when I pull up. You work for me two hours a day, five days a week. I want that wood back there stacked. I want the weeds cut and the grass mowed. I want my beans picked, the corn hoed. . . . Whatever I think of to be done, that's what you do. And I want you here startin' tomorrow."

"I'll be here," I says. "But I want it in writing that after I do twenty hours' work for you, Shiloh belongs to me."

Travers grunts and goes in his trailer. He comes out with a piece of grocery sack and the words "Beagle hunting dog to Marty Preston for twenty hours work. J. Travers."

It occurs to me suddenly that maybe after I

do the work, he'll try to pay me off with one of his other dogs.

"Write 'Shiloh,' " I tell him.

He gives me a pained look and crosses out "beagle," writes "Shiloh" in its place, but don't spell it right. Leaves off the "h" at the end.

I take the paper and put it in my pocket. "I'll be here tomorrow," I say.

"And you ever tell *anyone* about this deer, boy, you're going to be more'n sorry you opened your lips."

"You got my word," I say, which, considering all the lying I'd been doing lately, didn't seem like it amounted to much. It did, though.

I walk away from Judd's trailer in a sort of zigzag line, half expecting a bullet in my back any moment, even though I'm pretty sure he wouldn't. Soon as I'm out of sight, though, I race through the woods, heart going *thumpity-thump.* Can't keep the smile back no longer.

Shiloh's mine! The words keep coming back again and again. He's safe!

Should feel even more joyful, though. Thought once if I could just get Shiloh for my own, it would be the finest day of my life. In a way it is, in a way it isn't.

Could be Judd gave in 'cause he couldn't think

of nothing else at the moment to do. Said I could have Shiloh just 'cause he needed some help with that deer. Could be that once he got rid of the evidence, he'd tell me to go ahead and get the warden, that I wasn't to have the dog. Could even say he never wrote that on the grocery sack, that I'd wrote it myself.

I don't think so, though. What worries me most is that Judd could go through with the bargain, give Shiloh to me, but then someday, when Shiloh's running free in the woods by himself, Judd might put a bullet in his head, just to spite me.

CHAPTER 15

Closer I get to home, though, the bigger the grin on my face, and when I burst in the kitchen, I got a smile from ear to ear.

Dad's having his coffee and Ma's in the living room listening to the Sunday morning service by Brother Jonas. She watches him every Sunday at seven, which tells me what time it is already.

"Where you been?" says Dad, and I can tell Ma's paying attention, too. "You up and gone, we got to worrying."

I slide into my chair and almost have to push my cheeks in to keep the smile from going all the way around my head.

"Went to see Judd Travers," I say, still breathless, "and I'm buying his dog."

Ma gets up and comes to the kitchen doorway. "What?"

"Thought he wasn't selling," says Dad, looking at me hard.

"He wasn't, but I talked him into it. He needs

129

help around his place, and he says if I work hard for him for twenty hours, at two dollars an hour, that will pay the forty dollars he wants for Shiloh."

Ma's smile getting broader by the minute. "I don't *believe* it!" she says. "Shiloh's yours?"

"Not yet, but he will be, and we don't have to take him over to Judd's." Before I can get the last word out, she's got her arms around me, squeezing the breath from my chest, almost.

I think Shiloh can smell Judd Travers on me. He can smell the deer's blood, too; I know by the way he sniffs my shoes. But finally he just can't stand it no more. He's joyful I'm back, and he's lickin' me, welcoming me home.

But Dad's still studying my face. "I can't figure it, Marty. Judd seemed pretty definite about keepin' that dog. What was said between you?"

I really didn't want to lie no more. If I tell Ma and Dad everything except about the deer, that's lying by omission, Ma says: not telling the whole truth. But if I tell about the deer after promising Judd I wouldn't, then I would have lied to Judd. Rather lie to Judd than my folks, but I figure it this way: Dad wouldn't report Judd even if *he* saw him shoot a doe out of season, because that's the way it's always been around here. That don't necessarily make it right, of course, but with him feeling that way, nothing's going to change if I *do* tell him about Judd and the deer, and because I promised not to, I don't. Right now, the most important thing to me is Shiloh.

"Told him I wasn't going to give Shiloh back no matter what," I tell Dad.

They are sure staring at me now, him and Ma.

"You said that to Judd Travers?" Dad asked, scooting back in his chair.

"Only thing left to say. Only thing I could think of to do I hadn't tried already. Was going to tell him he could take me to court, and I'd tell the judge how he kicked his dogs. But didn't have to go that far. Guess he needs help around his place."

Ma turns to Dad. "You know, I think it's because Shiloh was hurt. I think he figures that dog's never going to be what it was, and that's why he was willing to let it go. Figured he got rid of a lame dog, and the best of the bargain, too."

"That's what I figure," I say.

And at last Dad begins to smile. "So we got ourselves a new member of the family," he tells me, and that's about the nicest thing I heard said in this house in my life.

Then Becky and Dara Lynn wakes up, sad faced 'cause they think we got to take Shiloh over to Judd's. I tell 'em the news, and Dara Lynn, she starts dancing. Becky joins in, whirling herself around, and then Shiloh, smiling his dog-smile, everybody whooping and carrying on.

Ma turns off the TV and makes waffles, with a big pat of margerine in the center of each one and hot homemade brown-sugar syrup filling the plates. She even makes a waffle for Shiloh. We're going to make that dog sick if we're not careful.

"Now all we got to worry about is how we can afford to feed him as well as ourselves," Dad says finally. "But there's food for the body and food for the spirit. And Shiloh sure enough feeds our spirit."

We about pet Shiloh to death. Everytime he turns around, someone's got a hand on him somewheres. I take him out for his first gentle run since he got hurt, and once up on the hill, him running free, the good feeling inside me grows bigger and bigger and I have to let it out. I hunch up my shoulders and go, "Heeeowl!"

Shiloh jumps and looks at me.

"Heeeowl!" I go again, out of joy and jubilation, the way they do in church. And suddenly Shiloh joins in with a bark. A pitiful kind of bark, like he's got to be taught how, but it's a happy bark, and he's learnin'.

Only bit of sadness left in me is for the deer. Wondering, too, about whose business it is when someone breaks the law. Wonder if Dad wouldn't never tell on Judd no matter what he done. Bet he would. There's got to be times that what one person does is everybody's business.

Monday afternoon at three o'clock, I'm waiting on Judd's porch when he pulls up. All his dogs is chained out to the side of the house, and they get to barkin' like crazy. I don't try to get near 'em, 'cause a chained dog can be mean. I've already restacked Judd's woodpile, but he wants me to do it again, put the big pieces here, the little ones there. He is looking mean and grumpy, like maybe he's disgusted with himself for lettin' me have that dog so easy.

When I finish the woodpile, Judd hands me the hoe. "You see that garden?"

I nod.

"You see that corn? I want the dirt chopped up so fine I can sift it through my fingers," he tells me.

Now I see what he's getting at. He's going to make it so there's no way I can please him. I'll put in my twenty hours and he'll tell me my work wasn't no good, he wants his dog back.

I hoe till I got blisters on both hands, sweat pouring down my back. Wish I could do my work in the early morning before the sun's so fierce. But I don't complain. I take off my T-shirt finally, wrap it around my head to keep the sweat out of my eyes, and

I keep on. Shoulders so red I know they'll hurt worse'n anything the next morning, and they do.

Next afternoon, Judd sets me to scrubbing down the sides of his trailer and his porch, shining up the windows, raking the yard. He sits on a folding chair in the shade, drinking a cold beer. Don't offer me nothing, even water. I hate him more than the devil. My mouth so dry it feels like fur.

Third day, though, he puts out a quart jar of water for me when I go to pick his beans. I bend over them rows so long, dropping the beans into a bucket, I think I'm going to be bent for life. When I'm through, Judd sort of motions me to the porch, like I can sit there if I want while I drink my water.

I almost fall onto that porch, glad to be in the shade.

"Looks like you got yourself some blisters," he says.

"I'm okay," I tell him, and take another long drink.

"How's Shiloh?" he asks. First time he's called the dog by that name.

"He's doing fine. Still got a limp, but he eats good."

Judd lifts his beer to his lips. "Would have been a good hunting dog if I could just have kept him home," he says. "The other dogs never run off."

I think about that awhile. "Well," I say finally, "each one is different."

"That's the truth. Kick one and he just goes under the porch for an hour. Kick another, he goes off and don't come back."

I'm trying my best to think what to say to that. Like how come he has to kick them at all? Then I figure nobody likes to be preached at, no matter how much he needs it, least of all Judd Travers, who is thirty years old if he's a day.

"Some dogs, it just makes 'em mean when you kick 'em," I say finally. "Other dogs, it makes 'em scared. Shiloh got scared."

"Never beat my dogs with a stick," Judd goes on. "Never did that in my life."

I don't say anything right away. Finally, though, I ask, "How *your* dogs doing?"

"Rarin' to go out rabbit hunting," Judd says. We look over at his three dogs, all pullin' at their chains and snarlin' at each other. "That biggest dog, now," Judd goes on. "He's the loudest squaller I got. I can tell from his racket whether he's following a fresh track or an old one, if he's runnin' a ditch, swimmin', or treed a coon."

"That's pretty good," I say.

"Littlest one, he's nothin' but a trashy dog— he'll run down most anything 'cept what I'm after.

Hope the others'll learn him something. And the middle dog, well, she gives a lot of mouth, too. Even barks at dead trees." The dogs were fighting now, and Judd throws his Pabst can at 'em. "You-all shut up!" he yells. "Hush up!"

The can hits the biggest dog, and they all scatter.

"Don't much like bein' chained," Judd says.

"Guess nobody would," I tell him.

I put in ten hours that week, meaning I make up twenty of the dollars I owe him; got one more week to go. When I leave of an afternoon for Judd's, Shiloh goes with me just so far, then he gets to whining and turns back. I'm glad he won't go on with me. Don't want him anywhere near Judd Travers.

Monday of the second week it seem like Judd's out to break my back or my spirit or both. This time he's got me splittin' wood. I got to roll a big old piece of locust wood over to the stump in his side yard, drive a wedge in it, then hit the wedge with a sledgehammer, again and again till the wood falls apart in pieces to fit his wood stove. Then another log and another.

I can hardly get the sledgehammer up over my head, and when I bring it down, my arms is so wobbly my aim ain't true. Almost drop the hammer. This ain't a job for me, and if Dad saw what Judd was makin' me do, he'd tell him it wasn't safe.

But Judd's out to teach me a lesson, and I'm out to teach him one. So I keep at it. Know it takes me twice as long as Judd to split that wood, but I don't stop. And all the while, Judd sits on his porch, drinking his beer, watching me sweat. Sure does his heart good, I can tell.

Then he says somethin' that almost stops my heart cold. Laughs and says, "Boy, you sure are puttin' in a whole lot of work for nothin'."

I rest my back a moment, wipe one arm across my face. "Shiloh's somethin'," I tell him.

"You think you're goin' to get my dog just 'cause you got some handwritin' on a piece of paper?" Judd laughs and drinks some more. "Why, that paper's not good for anything but to blow your nose on. Didn't have a witness."

I look at Judd. "What you mean?"

"You don't even know what's legal and what's not, do you? Well, you show a judge a paper without a witness's signature, he'll laugh you right out of the courthouse. Got to have somebody sign that he saw you strike a bargain." Judd laughs some more. "And nobody here but my dogs."

I feel sick inside, like I could maybe throw up. Can't think of what to do or say, so I just lift the sledgehammer again, go on splittin' the wood.

Judd laughs even harder. "What are you, boy?

137

Some kind of fool?" And when I don't answer, he says, "What you breakin' your back for?"

"I want that dog," I tell him, and raise the sledgehammer again.

That night when I'm sittin' out on the porch with Ma and Dad, Shiloh in my lap, I check it out. "What's a witness?" I say.

"Somebody who knows the Lord Jesus and don't mind tellin' about it," says Ma.

"No, the other kind."

"Somebody who sees something happen and signs that it's true," Dad says. "What you got in mind now, Marty?"

"You make a bargain with somebody, you got to have a witness?" I ask, not answering.

"If you want it done right and legal, I suppose you do."

I can't bear to have Dad know I was so stupid I made an agreement with Judd Travers without a witness.

"What you thinking on?" Dad asks again, hunching up his shoulders while Ma rubs his back.

"Just thinking how you sell something, is all. Land and stuff."

Dad looks at me quick. "You're not trying to sell off some of my land for that dog, are you?"

"No," I tell him, glad I got him off track. But I

sure am worried. Every trace of that deer's gone now. Don't know what Judd done with the meat—rented him a meat locker somewhere, maybe. But there's no bones around, no hide. I report him now, I can't prove a thing.

Next day Judd Travers calls me dumb. Sees me waiting for him on his steps and says I must have a head as thick as a coconut; didn't he already tell me that the paper wasn't worth nothing?

I just look straight through him. "You and me made a bargain," I say, "and I aim to keep my part of it. What you want me to do today?"

Judd just points to the sledgehammer again and doubles over laughin', like it's the biggest joke he ever played on somebody in his life. I can feel the sweat trickle down my back and I ain't even started yet.

Four o'clock comes, and I finally finished all that wood, but Judd pretends he's asleep. Got his head laid back, mouth half open, but I know it's just another way he's got to trick me. Wants me to sneak on home; then he'll say I never kept to my part of the bargain. So I go in his shed, put the sledgehammer back, take out the sickle, and go tackle the weeds down by his mailbox. Work on them weeds a whole hour, and when five o'clock comes, I start back toward the shed. See him watching me. I walk over.

"Sickle's gettin' dull, Judd. You got a whetstone around, I could sharpen it for you."

He studies me a good long while. "In the shed," he says.

I go get it, sit out on a stump, running the whetstone over the blade.

"Past five o'clock," says Judd.

"I know," I say.

"I ain't going to pay you one cent more," he says.

"It's okay," I tell him. Never saw a look on a man's face like I see on his. Pure puzzlement is what it is.

Thing I decide on when I head for Judd's again the next day is that I got no choice. All I can do is stick to my side of the deal and see what happens. All in the world I can do. If I quit now, he'll come for Shiloh, and we're right back where we started. I don't want to make him mad. No use having a winner and loser, or the bad feelings would just go on. Don't want to have to worry about Shiloh when he's running loose and I'm in school. Don't want to feel that Judd's so sore at me he'll think up any excuse at all to run his truck over my dog.

Only sign in this world we're making progress is the water Judd puts out for me. This day it even has ice in it, and Judd don't say one more word about a witness. In fact, when I'm through working and sit down on his porch to finish the water, Judd talks a little more than usual. Only bond we got between us is dogs, but at least that's somethin'.

I decide to say something nice to Judd. Tell him how good-looking his dogs are. Givin' a compliment to Judd Travers is like filling a balloon with air. You can actually see his chest swell up.

"Forty, thirty, and forty-five," he says, when I tell about his dogs.

"Those are their names now?"

"What I paid for 'em," he says.

"If they had a little more meat on their bones, I figure they'd be the best-lookin' hounds in Tyler County," I tell him.

Judd sits there, turnin' his beer around in his hands, and says, "Maybe could use a bit more fat."

I nurse my water along a little, too. "When'd you first get interested in hunting?" I ask him. "Your pa take you out when you was little?"

Judd spits. Didn't know a man could drink beer and chew tobacco at the same time, but Judd does. "Once or twice," he says. "Only nice thing about my dad I remember."

It's the first time in my life I ever felt anything like sorry for Judd Travers. If you weighed it on a postal scale, would hardly move the needle at all, but

I suppose there was a fraction of an ounce of sorry for him somewhere inside me. When I thought on all the things I'd done with my own dad and how Judd could only remember hunting, well, that was pretty pitiful for a lifetime.

Thursday, when I get there, Judd's meanness has got the best of him again, because I can see he's running out of work for me to do, just giving me work to make me sweat. Dig a ditch to dump his garbage in, he says. Hoe that cornfield again, scrub that porch, weed that bean patch. But close on to five o'clock, he seems to realize that I'm only going to be there one more time. I'd worked real hard that day. Did anything he asked and done it better than he asked me to.

"Well, one more day," Judd says when I sit down at last with my water and him with his beer. "What you going to do with that dog once he's yours?"

"Just play," I tell him. "Love him."

We sit there side by side while the clouds change places, puff out, the wind blowin' 'em this way and that. I'm wondering how things would have turned out if it hadn't been for that deer. If I'd just knocked on Judd's front door two weeks ago and told him I wasn't giving Shiloh up, what would have happened then?

To tell the truth, I think Ma's right. Judd would have sold him to me by and by because of Shiloh's limp. Judd's the kind that don't like that in a dog, same as he don't want a dent or a scratch of any kind on his pickup truck. Makes him look bad, he thinks. His truck's got to be perfect, to make up for all the ways Judd's not.

The last day I work for Judd, he inspects every job I do, finds fault with the least little thing. Keeps pesterin' me, makin' me hang around, do my work over. When it's time to go, I say, "Well, I guess that's it then."

Judd don't answer. Just stands in the doorway of his trailer looking at me, and then I get the feeling he's going to tell me I can take that paper he signed and use it for kindling. Tell me I can call the game warden if I want, there's not a trace of that deer left. The two weeks of work I put in for him was just long enough for rain to wash away the blood, for the field grass to spring back up again where the deer was shot.

He still don't say anything, though, so I start off for home, chest tight.

"Just a minute," says Judd.

I stop. He goes back inside the trailer, me waiting there in the yard. What am I going to say, he tries that? What am I going to do?

And then Judd's back in the doorway again, and he's got something in his hand. Comes down the steps halfway.

"Here," he says, and it's a dog's collar—an old collar, but better than the one Shiloh's got now. "Might be a little big, but he'll grow into it."

I look at Judd and take the collar. I don't know how we done it, but somehow we learned to get along.

"Thanks a lot," I tell him.

"You got yourself a dog," he says, and goes inside again, don't even look back.

I get home that evening, and Ma's baked a chocolate layer cake to celebrate—a real cake, too, not no Betty Crocker.

After dinner, Ma and Dad on the porch, the four of us rolls around on the grass together—Dara Lynn, Becky, Shiloh, and me. Becky tries to give Shiloh her butterfly kiss, but he don't hold still long enough to feel her eyelashes bat against him, just got to lick everywhere on her face.

And long after Becky and Dara Lynn goes inside, I lay out there on my back in the grass, not caring about the dew, Shiloh against me crosswise, his paws on my chest.

I look at the dark closing in, sky getting more and more purple, and I'm thinking how nothing is as simple as you guess—not right or wrong, not Judd Travers, not even me or this dog I got here. But the good part is I saved Shiloh and opened my eyes some. Now that ain't bad for eleven.

Boys against girls—double the fun!

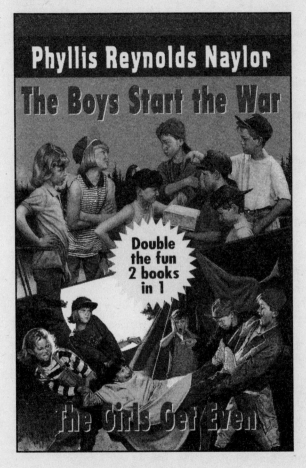

Available from Yearling Books

0-440-40971-3

Excerpt from *The Boys Start the War* by Phyllis Reynolds Naylor

Copyright © 1993 by Phyllis Reynolds Naylor

Published by Bantam Doubleday Dell Books for Young Readers,
Bantam Doubleday Dell Publishing Group, Inc.,
1540 Broadway, New York, New York 10036.

▼▲▼▲▼▲▼▲▼▲▼▲▼▲▼▲▼▲▼

One

▼

The Aliens

"The island's sinking!"

Wally studied the rivers of yellow that began streaming out from the middle.

"Sandbags! Sandbags!" he cried, lifting his waffle up at the edges with his fork, first one side, then the other.

If he made a little cut in each corner, the hot syrup traveled from one square to the next, but if he poured the syrup directly over the pat of butter, sitting like an island in the middle of his breakfast, the island grew smaller and smaller as the butter melted, until finally . . .

"They're coming!"

The back door banged and Wally jumped. Jake and Josh came tumbling into the kitchen, followed by seven-year-old Peter.

"Who?" asked Wally.

"The new guys over in Bensons' house!" Jake

1

grabbed the field glasses from the shelf where Mother kept them after she finished her bird-watching. "C'mon!"

Feet pounded on the stairs, and Wally knew that his brothers were headed for the trapdoor in the attic ceiling and the small balcony on top of the house—the widow's walk, it was called—where they could see out over the whole town, practically.

He sighed, picked up his plate and fork, and went up the first flight of stairs to the bedrooms, then the second set of stairs to the attic.

He could never understand why his two older brothers were always in such a rush. Sooner or later they would find out whether the three new boys in that family were their own ages or not, so why the hurry? Wally felt that you should spend the last week of summer vacation as lazily as possible, and now he couldn't even enjoy his waffle in peace.

Yesterday Josh had been sitting under a tree sketching Martians, or what he thought Martians would look like. Jake had been figuring out what they would all do on Halloween, and Wally and Peter had been lying in the grass, watching ants crawling in and out of a rotten apple—exactly the kinds of ways you expected to spend a summer day. Peter was the only one in the family who liked to study things the way Wally did. They both had brown hair, blue eyes, and thick, sturdy hands like their father's. Jake and Josh, however, were string-bean skinny, with skin that tanned by the first week of June.

1

Jake already had the stepladder in place, and Josh climbed to the top and pushed up on the trap-door. Blue sky shone through the square opening as a shower of pigeon droppings rained down on them. One piece landed on Wally's waffle. One gray-white blob of digested worms and bugs. Wally stared helplessly at his plate, then set it on the floor and followed his brothers to the balcony above.

He sat down in one corner and watched as Jake inched forward on his stomach, field glasses in hand, until he was close to the railing. The wind whipped at Wally's shirt, but it was a warm, dry wind that spelled September.

"Why are they just sitting there?" Jake wondered aloud, holding the glasses steady as he stared across the river.

Wally squinted, studying the car in the driveway of the house at the end of Island Avenue. The large piece of land in the middle of Buckman was not really an island, because water surrounded only three sides of it, but people called it "The Island" anyway. If you were coming in from the east, you entered Buckman on Island Avenue and kept going until you were out on the very tip, and then you crossed the bridge over into the business district. You might not even have noticed that the river on your right was the same as that on your left; it simply looped about at the end of the island.

"Okay, a door's opening, here they come!" said Jake.

"How old are they?" Josh asked.

Wally hoped there would be friends for each of them—an eleven-year-old for the twins, a nine-year-old for him, and a seven-year-old friend for Peter. The family that had moved out of the house on the other side of the river—who had left West Virginia to go to Georgia—had five boys of all ages, and they had been the best friends the Hatfords ever had.

"Well, say something!" demanded Peter when Jake didn't answer. "Are they aliens or what?"

"There's the father," said Jake. "Now someone's getting out one of the back doors. . . . A guy about twelve, I'd guess. . . ."

"Yea!" cheered Josh.

"No, wait a minute . . . it's a girl . . . no, a boy . . ." Jake's voice began to fade. "A girl. She just took off her cap."

A girl! Wally and Josh stared at each other. Who said anything about girls?

Josh took the field glasses next. He sat with his elbows propped on his knees, staring across the river. "No one else is getting out. . . . Now the other door's opening. It's the mother. . . . Here come the rest." He gasped. "Another girl . . . !"

"*Two* girls?" wailed Jake.

Wally thoughtfully bit his lip. This *was* serious! He grabbed the field glasses himself. "My turn," he said.

At the tip of the island a man and woman stood looking up at a large old house. Wally could see a

4

tall girl behind them, leaning against a tree and holding a baseball cap in one hand. A smaller girl was running down to the river.

Another leg emerged from the backseat of the car. A sneakered foot, faded jeans, a knee, a thigh, and then the last member of the new family got out and stretched.

"A girl," said Wally, disbelieving, and handed the field glasses back to Josh.

Nobody spoke for almost a minute.

"They're aliens, all right," said Josh.

"Three kids in one family and they're all girls?" Jake cried incredulously. "I thought Mrs. Benson told Mom they had rented their house to a family with three boys!"

Wally tried to remember exactly. "She said she thought there were three kids—"

"And that maybe we would still have enough to play baseball. . . ." added Josh. "*I* thought she meant *boys*!"

Wally's shoulders slumped. For years, ever since he could remember, the Hatford and Benson boys had got together every afternoon, rain or shine, to shoot BBs, fish, swim, play kick-the-can, camp out near Smuggler's Cove, climb Knob Hill, explore the old coal mine, or just lie on their backs in the grass and talk.

More than that, with the five Benson boys, the Hatford brothers regularly won first place in the costume contest at Halloween. One year they had each dressed up like some of the teachers at school; another year they had been dominoes; and a third year they chained themselves together like a prison gang. With the nine of them they had their own baseball team, and every May played a team from Grafton. They had even started their own band. Nothing would be the same again.

Wally stared out over the hills that dipped and rose like a roller coaster all around Buckman. The steeples of the United Methodist Church and the college chapel peeped up over the tops of the trees surrounding the courthouse, and the shiny horseshoe of a river curved around the island. It was a wonderful old town, but anytime he and his brothers walked over the swinging footbridge now, they would find three girls in the last house on Island Avenue, not the friends they had known all their lives.

"We just figured it would be a family of boys, that's all," he said at last.

"Well, we figured wrong," said Josh.

For a long while there was not another sound from the widow's walk. Finally Jake broke the silence:

"Let's burn the bridge."

Wally turned and stared. "What?"

"Just go down there some night and burn the footbridge," Jake said. "Then the girls couldn't get over to our side of the river. Not here, anyway.

They'd have to cross the road bridge and get to school the long way around."

"Don't be dumb," said Josh. "Dad would kill us."

"We don't have to burn the bridge. We'll just never invite them over here," said Wally.

"That's not enough," said Jake.

"We won't have anything to do with them," offered his twin, whose arms and legs were as long and spidery as Jake's.

"Not enough," said Jake.

"Well, what *do* you want to do, then? Vaporize them?" asked Peter, getting right to the point.

Jake sat with his lips pressed hard together and Wally could almost see currents connecting in his brain. Jake was the ringleader, the planner, and he usually got his way. "Do you remember the movie we saw once, *The Gang from Reno*?"

"Yeah," said Josh and Wally.

"No," said Peter.

"It was about this village up in the mountains," Jake told him. "A motorcycle gang from Reno comes and takes over. But the villagers finally drive them out just by making them miserable. We've got to make the new people miserable."

Wally leaned against the railing and studied Jake. It sounded pretty awful, even talking about it. "How do you know that the Bensons will move back if we do?"

"Because they weren't sure they'd like Georgia,

1

so they're only renting out their house here instead of selling. If they have trouble keeping renters, they just might give up and move back. You *know* they'd really rather live here. *Any*body would rather live here. We're just helping them make up their minds, that's all."

"But how are we going to make the new family miserable?" asked Josh, and they all turned to Wally. This always happened. Wally got involved whether he wanted to or not. He always said the first thing that came to his head, and that's why his brothers asked him.

"*Think*, Wally!" said Jake. "Think of the most terrible, awful, disgusting, horrible thing in the world."

Wally tried. He wondered if there was anything more awful or disgusting than pigeon poop on a waffle.

"Dead fish," he said finally.

Jake and Josh looked at each other.

"That's it!" yelped Josh. "We could dump them on the bank over on the other side, and the family will think the river's polluted."

"We'll dump everything dead we can find, and they'll be afraid to swim or fish or anything," said Jake. "Start collecting all the dead stuff you can, and put it in a bag in the garage. Great idea, Wally!"

"Hoo boy!" cried Josh. "The war is on!"

"Wow!" said Peter.

Wally blinked. How had this happened? What

8

had become of his wonderful day? Only a few minutes ago he'd been peacefully planning to float a waffle box down the river—see if it would make the curve at the end of Island Avenue and come back up the other side. Then he was going to climb to the top of the courthouse to see if there really were bats up there, the way Josh said, and after that he was going to jump from the largest branch of the sycamore into the river, and maybe he would even have gone out to the cemetery after dark, just to say he'd been.

He waited his turn at the trapdoor and slowly climbed down the ladder to the attic below. He picked up his plate, went down to the kitchen, scrunched up the empty waffle box and his waffle along with it, and then, with a sigh, threw them both in the trash.